AMAZING
GRACE NEWTON
and THE MISSING NOODLE

AMAZING
GRACE NEWTON
and THE MISSING NOODLE

N. JANE QUACKENBUSH

For information regarding permission, write to:
Attention: Hidden Wolf Books
155 West Genung St., St. Augustine, FL 32086

Copyright © 2018 by N. Jane Quackenbush
All rights reserved.
Published in the United States by Hidden Wolf Books.

ISBN 9780999434581
Library of Congress Control Number: 2018949970

Text set in Adobe Garamond

Version 1.1
Printed in the United States of America
First edition paperback printed, December 2018

To my family and friends.

Special thanks to
Kika Iadanza for her laser beams,
Joan Pospichal-LeBoss for rereading,
and my beautiful mother for her everything.

To: Clara
Stay Amazing!

∞ One ∞

Time To Fly

"Grace, it's time for bed," Momma called from the front porch.

"Yes, ma'am," I said as Mazie and I waved goodnight to one another.

"Who were you waving to?" Momma asked.

"Mazie," I said casually as I stepped inside our fragrant blossoming treehouse.

Momma shrugged then scooted me up the stairs.

I went straight to my room to say goodnight

1

to Noodle who sometimes spent his late afternoons taking naps on my bed, but he wasn't there. *Well, it was much too late for a nap,* I thought.

I peeked under the bed and into the closet … no Noodle. I looked inside Hope's and Abel's rooms … no Noodle. I searched in my parents' room … no Noodle.

Even though Noodle had free range of our home, he had a special cage that was kept in the mudroom. I ran downstairs and looked inside it, but it was empty. I couldn't find Noodle anywhere.

Where was Noodle?

"Momma!!! Noodle is missing!!!"

Papa came up and put his hand on my shoulder. "Grace, honey, I don't know how to tell you this, but Noodle's flown the coop."

I tried to understand what Papa was saying, but I had never heard that expression before. "What do you mean?"

"It means that Noodle went missing two days after you left … to go look for you … maybe."

"Noodle flew away to look for me?"

"I think so. I mean you should have seen the way he acted. It was not like Noodle at all."

"How did he act?"

"Like he missed you."

"Oh … poor Noodle," I looked away and imagined Noodle crying. *I didn't leave you, Noodle! I was just on an RV trip*, I telepathically said to him. "Did you look for him?"

"Yes, of course! We asked around but no one had seen a dressed chicken on the loose. Noodle will probably come back soon with you being back home and all. C'mon, let's get you ready and into bed, and we'll do another search in the morning, okay?"

"Okay," I said as I went to the bathroom to brush my teeth. I looked at myself in the old, pitted mirror. I was still wearing my grungy camping clothes—Hope's hand-me-down shorts and one of Alice's "clean" tie-dye t-shirts. I hadn't looked at myself in what seemed like forever. I looked so much more mature after our trip. It may be that I was extra tired though.

After a quick bath, Papa tucked me into bed and said, "I sure am glad you youngins are home. This stumpy old treehouse echoed too loudly without your voices to fill it. Plus, I missed you." Papa wrapped his fingers around my nose and stole it. "Got your nose!" He held his thumb in between his fingers as I giggled.

"Hey! Give me back my nose," I played along.

He put his thumb on my neck pretending to sniff me. *Sniff, sniff. sniff, sniff …*

"You smell like campfires!" he said.

"How'd you know?"

"How could I not know? If I didn't know any better, I'd think you were Smokey Bear!"

That reminded me. "We did see a bear!" My eyes grew wide as I recounted the story of how Mr. Box shooed away the pesky bear who was trying to break open Ol' Tex to get to us.

"Mr. Box?"

"Actually, his name is Benjamin Franklin Box, and he didn't have a name until he was eighteen, when he became a Marine."

"A Marine? Well, now, that is something special. Where did you meet him?"

"He was our neighbor at Camp Igottapoopie."

Papa laughed. "Camp I gotta-*what*?"

"Actually, the real name is Camp Bushpea, but everyone calls it Camp Igottapoopie, at least that's what Mr. Morsel called it."

"Wow, you must have met all kinds of people on your trip! Mr. Box, Mr. Morsel, who else?"

"Hope met a boyfriend," I said casually, trying to recall all the people we had met.

Papa's eyes weren't happy, suddenly. "We'll just see about that," he said as he finished tucking me in, gave me a kiss on my forehead, then stood to go.

"Are you mad?" I asked.

He looked back at me as he stood in the doorway, the tenderness returning to his eyes. "Don't grow up too fast, ya hear?"

✿ *Two* ✿

Artwork

I looked up at the gnarled wooden ceiling, noticing the scrape marks that were likely made by my great grandparents. We Newtons lived inside a living tree. It may have technically died hundreds of years ago, but its spirit remained intact within the trunk and our family, who kept it vibrant and growing. It reminded me of Nana. She may have technically died, but her spirit was still alive living inside all of us.

Whenever I remembered the times we had spent sewing, baking cookies, and dancing together, Nana still lived inside my thoughts and imagination. As soon as we arrived home from our trip, I could feel her presence much stronger than when we were RVing. It felt good to be near her again, even though I couldn't see her.

My eyes landed on my nightlight as I heard Momma getting Aunt Esther and Alice's sleeping situations worked out.

"We could just stay in the cabin, you know," Aunt Esther said, not wanting to make Momma do any more work than necessary.

"I know, but stay here for at least tonight," Momma said. "I like having you here with me."

As I drifted off to sleep, I wondered where Noodle was. Was he traveling over the river and through the woods using his tracking skills to find me? Was he back at Camp Igottapoopie with Mr. Box and Scoops? If so, would Mr. Box recognize him and send him back home? Or would Mr. Box deliver Noodle himself?

That night I dreamed that Noodle had a baby. In my head I knew it was impossible, but in the dream it seemed so real. Papa was a boy, and he had three babies, Hope, me, and Abel. So why couldn't Noodle have a baby? He was in a big barn filled with lots of other chickens.

Noodle was the only chicken wearing overalls so he was easy to spot. I ran over to him but he didn't seem to recognize me so I lifted him up to give him a hug. Instead, he wanted to be put down so he could be near his baby.

When I woke in the morning, I heard Smith and Wesson's rooster crowing. That rooster was a lot closer than usual. I rolled out of bed smelling the coffee brewing from downstairs. As I padded down the smooth spiral stairs, I felt the fine lines along the velvety wooden walls.

Alice's eyes were not quite open as she was sitting at the table sipping on a steaming hot cup of coffee. "Mornin'," she said.

"Morning," I said back.

"You look like you could use a cup of Joe," she said as vapor rose from her cup, eventually disappearing.

"Is Joe hot chocolate?"

Alice smiled, shaking her head, then repositioned and said, "Oh, you want a Cocoa Joe!"

"What's that?" I asked.

"Hot chocolate."

My eyes squinted happily as I nodded.

"One Cocoa Joe coming right up," Aunt Esther said as she was coming out of the pantry holding a bag of flour in one hand and a canister

9

of chocolate powder in the other.

I licked my lips as Aunt Esther was melting butter in the pan and whipping up some pannekakas for everyone. The kettle whistled. Hot water was poured into a mug, then topped off with some fresh whipped cream. What a way to start the day!

One by one, everyone came down to eat Aunt Esther's beautiful, buttery breakfast of maple syrup topped pannekakas, sliced strawberries, and oven baked bacon. I lapped the bacon around in the syrup before I dangled it into my mouth.

Mmm-mmm.

"So, what's the plan for today?" Aunt Esther asked.

Without thinking for one second, I blurted, "Find Noodle."

"How do you suppose we do that?" Aunt Esther asked.

"We can make posters," I said.

"I'll help you," Hope said, much to my amazement. "Do we have any bright colored paper?"

Papa was giving Hope a certain kind of look that Hope refused to meet. I could sense some tension.

"I have some under my bed," Abel said as he played with his bacon.

Hope and I excused ourselves then ran up the swirly stairs looking for Abel's art supplies. We found a good selection of paper, crayons, markers, and glue. As we were arranging them in some kind of order, Hope asked, "Why did you tell Papa?"

Somehow, I knew what Hope was asking, but I needed a second to think of the right way to respond. Hope was sometimes too smart for me, and if I answered her the wrong way, it could result in her being mad or terribly disappointed in me.

"About what?" I asked.

"You know what! Now, he thinks we need to have a serious talk, and I'm not ready for that!"

I had no idea what kind of serious talk Papa wanted to have with Hope. I mean, all in all, I knew Stefan was harmless. But papas saw things differently, I guess. I wasn't sure how to proceed with Hope. Should I apologize? Should I pretend that I didn't know what she was talking about?

"Look, Grace, let's make a deal. I will help you with these posters if you will help me."

"How can I help you?"

"If or when Papa wants to have that talk with me, will you vouch for me and tell him that Stefan was just a friend and not a 'boyfriend'?" Hope wrapped air quotes around the word boyfriend.

I did the same when I asked, "Is Stefan your 'boyfriend'?"

"That's not your concern; all you need to know is that he was just a boy that we met at camp … nothing more than that."

"Okay, so you want me to lie?" I asked, willing to lie for her if she was willing to help me find Noodle. I knew lying was wrong, and it very much is wrong, but kids aren't always perfect.

"It's not lying!" Hope became agitated.

"So, Stefan isn't your boyfriend?"

Hope rolled her eyes. "Like I said before … not your concern. Just say that he was a friend, and that's all. That is the truth. He was a boy, and he became a friend."

"Did you kiss him?"

"Grace! Seriously!" Hope blushed. "Don't ask any more questions. Let's just find your stupid chicken."

"Hey! Noodle's not stupid!"

Abel ran in with his cape draped over his back. He picked up Milkshake, his big brown stuffed horse, and pretended to ride it around then stopped while waving Milkshake's front legs, rearing in the air like it was a wild stallion. "Super Abel is here to save the day!"

"Okay, Super Abel, come use your superpowers to make some 'Missing Noodle' posters. Can you draw a chicken in overalls?" Hope asked.

"No problem!" Abel assured her.

"Great, here are your supplies." She handed him a stack of paper and some crayons.

We doodled away our morning making not so great attempts at capturing Noodle's chickenness. Hope was the winner of the neatness competition. Abel was the winner of the most unlikely to find Noodle award. I was the winner of the best drawn chicken award, but none of ours were actually spectacular. Either way, we had to go find Noodle.

✺ *Three* ✺

Bomb Berry Pie

We set off with a stack of fresh posters, tape, and a staple gun that only Hope was allowed to use. We walked around town asking shop owners, the mailman, and police officers if they had seen Noodle. I held up my drawing for them, but, unfortunately, our questions produced only smiles and shaking heads because no one had seen my Noodle.

My detective-like nose was picking up on a scent. It was sweet, delicious, and very different from Noodle's bouquet that was much more fowl in nature. Okay, maybe what I was smelling was a heavenly aroma spilling out from Easy as Pie, a quaint little bakery across the street from where we stood. The pink and black awning waved in the breeze, inviting us to enter. How could we resist?

Tinkle bells rang as we opened the bakery door. A sweet, icy scent rushed up our nostrils as we entered the brick-floored, old fashioned bakery. A wall of antique pitted mirrors stood behind cases of beautifully decorated towering cakes.

I put on the guise of detective just to get the business part of our investigation to rest before I might stare and drool over the cakes that I could not afford. I held up my drawing of Noodle and asked, "Have you seen my pet chicken, Noodle?"

"No, I'm so sorry!" Ms. Nilla who owned the bakery said as she was wiping some frosting off her fingertips onto her apron. "I haven't seen your bird, but I do have an extra three slices of 'bomb berry' pie; would y'all each like a piece?"

"Sure!" Abel, who never ate voluntarily, said.

We didn't have any money on us, and we were told by our parents never to beg, but that pie sure did look delicious.

Hope and her hungry eyes spoke in an unconvincing tone for us. "Thank you, ma'am, but we better be on our way." Just as she was speaking, an obvious gurgle echoed from my belly.

"Now, y'all can't be searching for your pet chicken all day then go all the way back up to your place on an empty belly now, can y'all?"

We politely shook our heads as I resisted screaming out, *PIE!!! ME want PIE!!!*

Ms. Nilla started cutting pieces while saying, "This pie is my treat. Now, sit down here, and I'll get it ready for y'all."

Thank goodness she offered. I wanted it so badly! I hushed my grumbly belly that was eager about its upcoming arrival and readied my teeth to sink into a sweet exploding bomb berry pie. Ms. Nilla gave of us each a glass of sweet tea, a napkin, and a fork before she set a plate of bomb berry pie, oozing with buttery cinnamon, topped with whipped cream in front of us.

Abel attempted to form the cream into some kind of sculpture, but Hope quietly scolded him, "Abel, you can't play with Ms. Nilla's food. Eat it and don't be rude."

Abel looked over to Ms. Nilla who gave him

a twinkle. Next, he stabbed the triangular tip then shoved it into his little mouth, chomping on the pie with a smile. He giggled. Obviously, he liked it.

I rubbed my quiet stuffed stomach after I had lapped up every crumb and slurped away each delectable drop. When I went to lick the plate, Hope shook her head, stopping me from looking like a doofus.

"Grace, wipe your mouth. You have pie all over your lips."

"Oopsies," I said as I tried to clean the pie off my face, but nothing could wipe away my smile.

"Looks like y'all liked my bomb berry pie!"

"I've never tasted anything so scrumptious," Abel said as Hope and I blushed at his unexpected statement.

"Thank you, Ms. Nilla. Abel is right. Your pie is beyond scrumptious, but we better get back to our search party," Hope said as Ms. Nilla took our dishes.

"Well, I'm sure you'll find your chicken, now that y'all have full bellies."

She smiled and waved goodbye as the tinkly bells rang when we opened the door. "Goodbye," we said.

"Bye, now," she said.

On our way home, we stapled the fliers to some power poles at important intersections. I figured if Noodle was out looking for me, he had probably passed this way before. And somebody had to have seen him as he strutted along these lonely mountain roads. It's not every day you see a chicken crossing the road, wearing overalls.

AMAZING GRACE NEWTON

⚬ *Four* ⚬

Gathering Clues

"Any luck?" Aunt Esther asked as we were walking past Nana's cottage. She was sweeping off the front porch while Alice was shaking out some dusty rugs.

"Not yet," I said. Abel's acceleration button must have been pushed because suddenly he took off up the hill as if somebody was chasing him.

"Where's he headed so quickly?" Alice smiled as she asked.

"Home, probably," Hope said.

"Why the hurry?" Alice asked.

"That's just how Abel walks—he runs," Aunt Esther said.

"I swear he's going to be in the Olympics one day." Alice nodded.

I heard the washing machine and dryer going from the porch and saw what looked like a deep cleaning underway. "Are you guys moving in to Nana's cabin?" I asked.

"Just temporarily … You know how we like to travel, but sometimes it's nice to be able to spread out," Aunt Esther said.

"I wish you would stay here forever," I said.

"Oh, Grace, that's the nicest thing you could have said. We weren't sure how you'd feel." Aunt Esther came over and gave me a hug. "I know how close you kids were to Nana. I want you to know, you will always be welcome to come do your sewing or even if you just want to come and sit here. Nana's cottage is and always will be open for all you kids."

"It was fun having you sleep over with us last night, especially the breakfast part." I said as I grinned.

Aunt Esther and Alice shared a smile before giving each of us a good long hug.

"Have you checked any of the neighboring farms?" Alice asked.

"For what?" I asked.

"Noodle."

"Oh!" I wasn't sure if Alice was talking about the breakfasts that other farms served. I'm sure they served some pretty good breakfasts, as well. Oh, I should probably answer her question now … "Actually, no. I didn't think to check the other farms for Noodle."

"That would be the first place that I would look. Chickens get lonely. They need friends. I bet she's just found some friends over at a neighboring farm."

"She?" I asked. "Noodle's a boy chicken."

Alice laughed. "That would make him a rooster, and when I saw your chicken …" she paused, … "That's the chicken you had dressed in overalls, right?"

"Yes," I said.

"She's a girl."

"Noddle's a girl?"

"Yup."

I looked over at Hope. "How come you never said anything?"

Hope gave me a bewildered look. "I never knew you thought Noodle was really a boy."

"He wore overalls! Not a dress!" I tried to plead my case.

"Girls wear overalls, too!" Hope said.

"Oh." She had a point there. Girls *do* wear overalls.

Hmmmm.

I was trying to rethink everything I had previously thought about Noodle. If Noodle was a girl, then *she* probably *was* lonely when I left to go RVing. So that must be it! She went to go look for a new friend. I thought and pictured the closest farm that could have chickens for Noodle to befriend.

… *Aha*!

AND THE MISSING NOODLE

⌀ *Five* ⌀
Spit Spot

"You need some help here?" Hope asked Aunt Esther and Alice as they were straightening and dusting every little trinket in Nana's cottage.

"No, we're fine, but since you asked, here's a duster for you and a broom for you," Alice said as she handed Hope the feathered wand and the broom to me.

Honestly, I really wanted to skedaddle and go investigate my hunch on Noodle's whereabouts, but since Aunt Esther and Alice had just taken us on one of the most memorable trips of a lifetime, I figured it was our duty to help them. But we could not work in silence … I put on one of Nana's records to help us get into the cleaning mood.

I danced with the broom as Hope dusted the furniture with that certain sassafras feeling that music gives you. Aunt Esther glided around the room, organizing it as Alice played percussion with the banging of the rugs. This homey, rustic cottage was getting "spit spot", as Nana had always termed it.

"Good job, girls! We really appreciate your help," Aunt Esther said as we were sitting down drinking a glass of lemonade after we had finished scrubbing, mopping, dusting, and spit spotting. I bet Nana would have been happy seeing her cabin sparkle. I thought back to the dream I had when Pixie Nana, in all her vivid vibrancy, had visited me after Hope and I had cleaned and decorated her boogie barn for her big life celebration. I knew it wasn't just a dream. I knew without a doubt that Nana had really visited me. I wondered if she would visit me again tonight.

The phone rang. Aunt Esther picked it up, greeted the caller, and said, "Yes, they're here. Uh-huh … yup … sure, I'll send them right up."

"Was that Momma?" I asked. I already knew because I could hear her voice. I knew my momma's voice anywhere.

"Yes, she wants you girls to get on home and help with dinner."

"A woman's work is never done, uh-hum," Alice sang.

"Ain't that the truth," I said before Aunt Esther and Alice shook their heads and laughed.

"C'mon, Grace, let's go," Hope said with unmistakable hints of exhaustion.

"I'm a comin' … you lead the way."

"We'll see you in a bit. We're going to get cleaned up first then head on over." Aunt Esther said.

✑ Six ✑

Bubble Therapy

Dusk was settling into the sky. The black silhouette of trees against an orange sky enveloped Hope and me as we tromped up the hill to our flower-filled, unsymmetrical, hollowed-out tree home. I couldn't help but look over at my twinkling tree that flashed silvery lights, reflecting my orangey-purple puddle's light as the sun set.

I made a slight detour over to see Mazie. "Hi!"

"Hi!"

"Did you have a nice day?" she asked.

"Well, yes and no."

"Okay, why yes?"

"Yes, because I got to eat pannekakas, bacon, bomb berry pie with fresh whipped cream, and I got to spend the day with Hope and Abel while looking for Noodle."

"Why no?"

"No, because I didn't find Noodle."

"Uh-oh," Mazie looked puzzled … exactly how I felt.

"But I have a hunch. I think I might know where h … I mean *she* is." It still felt funny saying she.

"Grace, c'mon!" Hope called from the porch. "Quit talking to that puddle! You look crazy." Hope slammed the screen door as she walked inside.

"Stop slamming the door!" Momma yelled.

I didn't care how I looked. I looked down at Mazie. Poor Mazie, I think Hope may have hurt her feelings because her face looked sad. "It's okay, Mazie. I don't care what Hope thinks. You're real to me."

Mazie smiled.

"I have to go, but I'll see you soon, okay?"

I said as I stood.

"Okay," she waved as I too waved goodbye.

• • •

"Well, any luck?" Papa asked as he came in holding Abel like he was an airplane flying through the house. "Find 'em?"

"No," Hope said. "Guess we'll have to set out extra early again tomorrow to look for that silly chicken."

Why was Hope suddenly so concerned about Noodle? She never seemed to notice my pet before.

"Papa, Noodle's a girl." I corrected him.

Papa cleared his throat while looking over at Momma. "Of course, he's a girl. I just got used to you saying 'him' all the time that I just went along with it, I guess." He shrugged.

"Grace, can you please set the table? Hope, will you fill everyone's glass with ice water?"

"Yes, Momma," we said as we got to work.

To start the table setting in a most delightful way, I found one of Nana's old hand-embroidered table clothes and spread it across. It was a lovely blue and yellow buttercup backdrop. Within the upper cabinets, I pulled out a stack of white dishes and set them around the table. I opened the silverware drawer, grabbed seven forks, knives, and spoons then arranged them to surround the plates. As Hope placed the full, clinking glasses of ice water around, I put the chicken wire napkin holder that was in the shape of an apple in the center of the table next to a pair of orange ceramic mushrooms that held the salt and pepper.

"What a pretty table!" Aunt Esther said as she and Alice came into the kitchen. Alice was being careful to not slam the screen door.

Momma looked at the table we had set and smiled. It was nice to see Momma's smile. I walked over and gave her a hug as she stirred.

"Oh, Poodle Poo … Thank you, honey. Momma loves you," she said as I hugged her wagging waist.

"Luf you, Momma," I said as I looked up at her warm brown eyes.

"I love you, too!" Abel joined in while Hope indignantly watched us compete for Momma's affection.

"It's time to eat!" Momma announced as Abel and I scurried away, plopping onto our chairs.

On the menu tonight was a variety of

freshly roasted garden vegetables, fried okra, eggplant, spaghetti squash noodles, and creamy cheesy tomato sauce.

"Grace, would you like to say a prayer over our dinner?" Momma asked.

Momma had never asked me to pray over our meals before; although, I had volunteered on occasion. I wasn't sure if Momma prayed ever. I had never heard her.

"Okay," I said as I bowed my head, put my hands together and asked for a blessing on our food.

Everything tasted so much better than it sounded. My momma must have thrown in an extra heaping amount of love into all of these dishes because they were so delectable. My face got extra messy as I slurped up those saucy, cheesy squash noodles.

"Grace, watch yourself. You're making a mess," Momma said.

"Oopsies," I said as I watched my family as they ate. Abel talked with his mouth full. Papa neatly placed each bite within his mustached mouth. Hope methodically moved food around on her plate before deciding which bite to take. Aunt Esther had a no nonsense approach to eating while Alice stuck her tongue out to usher

her food in like a conveyor belt. But Momma took her time eating, closing her eyes while she chewed.

She looked exhausted even though she looked genuinely happy, I could tell that she, like every day, had worked hard.

I got an idea!

I started to get up but then sat back down and asked. "Can I be excused?"

"Are you finished with your dinner?" Papa asked.

"Yes, I just need to clean off my face."

My face obviously looked as filthy as it felt. "Go ahead," Papa permitted.

I ran upstairs but didn't clean off my face at first. Instead, I turned the white porcelain knobs that stood above the claw-foot tub like an old-fashioned telephone in Momma's bathroom. I felt the toasty water, adjusting it to make sure it wouldn't be scalding. I poured a slick stream of pearlescent lavender liquid, getting a bubble bath ready for Momma. As I waited for the tub to fill, I lit some candles and placed them around the bathroom. What a great place to relax! I laid out a towel and washcloth, then called Momma upstairs.

"Momma, I need you to come up to

your room. I need to tell you something very important." You might think that was a lie, but it wasn't. I had to tell her that she had a relaxing bubble bath waiting for her … and that was super important.

When Momma came up the stairs, I heard her exhale. But when she came into her bathroom, she gasped.

"Is this for me?" she asked.

"Yes, Momma," I said.

"Oh, Grace, you are so thoughtful. But I have to clean up the kitchen then fold a load of laundry, and …"

I interrupted her. "No, Hope, Abel, and I will do all that. You just need to relax and unwind."

Momma exhaled. She looked around at the candlelit room and the tub full of warm bubbles then quietly said, "Thank you!"

"You need some R and R," I didn't exactly know what that meant but I had heard adults use that term when talking about needing some time off.

She looked tenderly into my eyes then said, "Okay, but you need to wipe the sauce off your face."

"Oopsies!" I had forgotten to clean

myself. I stole the washcloth that I had out for Momma, dunked it into the bath water, then wiped off my face. I checked in the mirror then back at Momma who was already neck deep in the bath.

"That was fast!" I said.

"I had to act quickly before I changed my mind," she said before she lowered her head beneath the bubbles.

AND THE MISSING NOODLE

༄ *Seven* ༄

Rematch

Hope, Aunt Esther, Alice, and I worked together to clean up the kitchen as Abel and Papa took out the stinky trash. We had an assembly line going. I scraped, Aunt Esther cleaned, Alice rinsed, while Hope dried and put away the dishes. Doing dishes with everyone made it go by quickly.

After the laundry was folded and the kitchen was sparkling clean, Aunt Esther and Alice were thumbing through some of our books, looking for something to read from the curvy book shelf that was carved into the other side of the spiral stairs. We had books that went back for generations. Aunt Esther pulled out a tiny shining book about the same size as her palm. When she opened it and read the inscription, she smiled slightly then showed Alice.

I glanced at the "growing wall" that had all of us Newtons's measurements throughout the years. By my last measurement, from a few months ago, I knew for sure that I had grown at least an inch or two—same with Abel and Hope. I felt so tall as I stood up straight while glancing at myself in the antique mirror on the opposite wall.

Alice grabbed a game of checkers and dared any one of us kids to challenge her. I never was able to beat Alice at checkers. She was too good. But that didn't mean I was too scared to try. Hope looked at me as I volunteered.

"You're not as chicken as I thought," Alice jeered.

"Noodle is a chicken. I'm a girl who is scared of *not* trying to beat you." I said.

Alice gave me a thoughtful look. "You know that's probably some of the wisest words I have ever heard. Grace, you never cease to amaze me. Now get over here and get ready to lose."

It was humiliating losing so badly right away, but Aunt Esther gave me some pointers and then … then … You're not to going to believe what I'm about to tell you … I won! I knew you wouldn't believe me, but I did it! I won fair and square. Okay, yes, I lost the first ten or so games, badly, but I finally won … one game. Believe me, I was just as shocked.

"Well, I never thought I'd see the day when someone beat Alice at something," Aunt Esther chuckled. "It's not every day that you can say that you beat a champion, much less an Olympian at something."

I was jumping around the parlor like a kangaroo. I ran in to the den to tell Papa and Abel who didn't seem to care that much. Hope looked somewhat amused, but no one shared the extreme excitement that I now housed within my soul. Aunt Esther was definitely excited so I'd put her at a close second, and if I didn't know any better, I'd bet that Alice was actually pretty happy for me even though it meant that she had lost.

After all of my obnoxious celebrating, I settled down as I walked into the parlor and dramatically plopped onto the chair next to Hope. Savory scents leftover from dinner gave our home a warm essence. There was a warm feeling traveling through our happy home. My ears picked up on a barely audible ringing from the television that echoed through the house as Papa and Abel were in the den watching some football videos. It was nice having all of my family under one roof.

"Only two more weeks of summer," Hope said as we lounged in the parlor.

"What?" I sprung up. "No! I don't want to go back to school." That warm comfortable feeling fizzled before my eyes.

"I can't wait to get back," Hope said as if school was cool or something.

"Why? What's so great about school?"

"Friends, a couple of fantastic teachers, and fun."

"Friends are fun, but I'm not sure about the rest."

"Don't you have a favorite teacher?"

I tried to recall all three of my teachers. Miss Spittle was my kindergarten teacher, and Mr. Dunckler was my first grade teacher. They were okay, but none stood out as my favorite.

"My favorite teacher was Dr. Wilde," Aunt

Esther said. "She was my college poetry teacher, and she taught me how to read."

"You didn't know how to read until you went to college?" Hope wondered.

"I knew how to fool people, but, actually, I was, I mean *am*, dyslexic. I read differently than most people."

"How so?" Hope asked.

"Well, for instance, when I see a word it looks different to me than to a person without dyslexia. So I had to learn to adjust the way my brain sees things so I could read and write like people who don't have dyslexia. Dr. Wilde noticed that I had gone my whole life without really knowing how to read. When she retaught me how to understand symbolic words and language, a whole new world opened up for me. It was like I went from flat vision to seeing words come alive in 3D."

"Oh, wow!" I said.

"After that, when I read books, it was like watching fantastic, colorful, mesmerizing movies inside my own head. These amazing authors painted pictures, worlds, and sceneries with words that my brain was able to fill in with my own unique point of view."

I thought back to when Aunt Esther and

Alice had read the "Indian Burial Mound" poem to me and how my mind was able to conjure its own images based on the clever descriptive words the author had used. And how Abel and I had thought that we had encountered a real life burial mound, but it was only where Stinky had been buried¾not an Indian.

A big ear-popping yawn overtook me before I noticed Momma gently padding down the stairs, wrapped in a fluffy pink robe with steam still emanating from her bathed skin. The way her eyes wilted and the graceful gait of Momma's steps let me know that the bubbles had done their job. Momma looked so peaceful. The stress that Momma appeared to have had earlier had gone down the drain.

"You look so relaxed, Ruth," Aunt Esther said.

"I feel so relaxed. Just getting a sip of water before bed." I heard her filling a glass with water then she walked in and gave me a certain look, "Grace, you look tired, too, honey. Would you like for me to read you a bedtime story?"

"Me?" I couldn't believe it. Momma was usually too busy doing chores, laundry, and what not … she almost never had time for a bedtime story.

"Yes, you."

AND THE MISSING NOODLE

৵ Eight ৵

Baby Eels

I jumped up, hastily said goodnight to everyone, ran upstairs, brushed my new stumpy teeth, then bounced into bed, waiting for Momma.

When I heard her steps coming, I got so excited. I saw her shadow shrinking as she got closer. I could smell the sandalwood bubble bath still spicing up her skin as she sat down on my bed. In her hand was a book that she used to read to me when I was younger. She sat quietly at first then looked around.

"I forgot how peaceful your room is," she quietly said.

Momma had decorated and painted the room a violet color soon after I was born. Red and yellow mushroom curtains flanked my window, giving it a tranquil forest feeling. The whimsical hand-carved wooden bed must have been enchanted because it always made me feel like I was sleeping in a fairytale. And the quilt Nana had made for me kept me covered in comfort all night.

Momma reached over and tugged on the chain to light my bedside lamp. My eyes took a second to adjust. When I opened them, Momma was looking at me.

"Grace, you're getting to be such a big girl! You know, I can remember when you were inside my belly." Momma rubbed her stomach and gave me a smile. "You were such an easy baby to carry. When I was pregnant with Hope, I got so big, I looked like a beach ball! But with you, I hardly put on any extra weight." Momma looked around then shrugged. "But maybe that's because I was already much heavier from having Hope."

"What about when you were pregnant with Abel?" I asked.

"Oh! Abel … I was so sick. I couldn't stop

throwing up! Don't you remember?"

I couldn't remember because I was so young when Abel was born.

"No," I said.

"Well, for some reason you were easy. I remember smiling a lot when I was pregnant with you. You had this great chemistry with my body, making me feel good. In fact, you still always make me feel good when you're near me ... Almost like a warm hot bubble bath." Momma winked.

I gushed with overwhelming gratitude at this enormous compliment. I always tried to make everyone feel better. Knowing that I was making the most important woman in my life feel that way, was simply serendipitous. I didn't even know what that word, serendipitous, meant but it just felt right, even if it wasn't.

Opening the book in her hands, she asked, "Ready?"

I nodded as she began to read:

Are You my Eel?
by Naja Q

On a bright sunny day at the bottom of the sea,
swum a certain special eel—a mother to be.

AMAZING GRACE NEWTON

Her belly full of babies and a smile on her face,
she lay her baby eggs in a super-secret space.

Tucked behind a rock, atop a bed of grass,
a lovely pile of eggs dropped into a crevasse.

Preoccupied and busy, doing motherly work,
an octopus took a scoop of her eels, like a jerk.

He stole her precious babies and sneakily swam away.
Mother Eel quickly followed, but lost
him along the way.

Mother Eel deplored to all who could hear,
"He stole all of my babies!" she said loud and clear.

No one was listening as she continued to explore.
Alas, she found a baby eel upon the ocean floor.

"Are you my eel?" the mother asked through
sodden tears;
When suddenly hope replaced all of her fears.

All was not lost, as she picked up her prize.
She placed him in a safer spot—for now,
she was wise.

AND THE MISSING NOODLE

She knew what could happen when
found unaware.
Baby safety was most important in her childcare.

She never left his side and cared for his every need;
Until the day her baby eel was older and weened.

The baby eel matured and left home, all alone.
No need for his mother—for he was all grown.

Sadly, she allowed him to make his own way,
Saying, "I'll always be here, Eel, if you need
me someday."

Mother Eel feared the coming of this day.
The other eels used reason to make it seem okay.

"It's what they're supposed to do," the other eels said.
"But that doesn't make it easy," Mother Eel plead.

Day after day, Mother found things to take up
her time;
With many things to do, the mother felt fine —
sort of.

But as Mother Eel grew older, she needed special care,
For she was all alone and no one was there.

A day never went by without thinking about her Eel.
Happily, he returned while she was eating a meal.

Surprised she was and hugged him bottom to top;
Kissed him ear to ear and wasn't going to stop.

Until she saw his family waiting by the door,
As they swam around in circles along
the ocean floor.

"Momma, here is my family, for they are
yours now, too."
Mother Eel was so excited, she didn't know
what to do.

She darted here and there, happy as can be.
For now, she truly had a great big family.

They lived happily ever after, Eel and his mother,
All together they thrived in family like no other.

The moral of the story is that your babies
grow up fast;
Never expect their youth to ever, ever last.

*Instead, be sure to hug them every single day.
You never know when you'll need them to come
back to stay.*

Momma had a little tear streaming down her face. "You kids are growing so fast! Makes me sad to think that one day you'll be on your own." Momma brushed my hair away from my face while looking tenderly into my eyes.

"Can I look at the pictures?" I asked.

Momma handed the book to me. I flipped through the pages looking at the words but mostly at the illustrations which made the words more understandable.

I had always loved this story, but since I had gone RVing with Aunt Esther and Alice and they had read to me, I realized that this story was a poem. It rhymed, and I liked how that sounded. I thought it was clever to be able to paint a picture with words but to make the words rhyme was quite extraordinary. I hadn't paid much attention to the words in books before. But when Alice and Aunt Esther explained them to me, stories made more sense. I didn't feel as dumb as I used to—when it came to books.

I must have looked a little too peaceful. My eyes struggled to stay open as Momma leaned over and gave me a kiss.

"Night, night Poodle Poo."

"Night, night, Momma," I yawned as I drifted off to sleep.

AND THE MISSING NOODLE

᦬ Nine ᦭

Detective Hope

Hope woke me up early in the morning. "Grace, c'mon we gotta get going."

"Huh? Where?"

"To go find Noodle."

"Oh," I sleepily said as I was noticing the sun barely over the horizon.

"Here, get dressed," Hope threw me a fresh outfit to wear which floated over and landed on my head. I pulled it over and slowly dressed myself.

When I went into the hallway, Hope rolled her eyes and said, "Your shirt's on backwards *and* inside out."

I looked down. "Oopsies," I said as I readjusted my shirt.

It was so early that Momma and Papa weren't even awake as we had walked downstairs. It felt strange being in the kitchen so early with no adults to warm it with breakfast.

"What about breakfast?" I asked, wishing that someone would hear my request for grub.

"Here's an apple." Hope reached into the fruit basket and gruffly handed it to me.

Not the grub I was looking for … "That's not enough," I said.

"If we're going to get an early start, it will have to do. You do want to find Noodle, don't you?"

"Yes, but …"

"Then let's go!" Hope trotted out of the screen door, careful, for the first time, to not let it slam.

Morning fog hung around the tree trunks like thick heavenly carpeting keeping nature hushed. A cool mist mixed with daytime's coming warmth filled my lungs from the crisp outdoor air—perfect sleeping weather.

I assumed Mazie was still sleeping when we passed by the quiet purple puddle. Nibbling on my apple, I sleepily followed Detective Hope wherever she was picking up on Noodle's scent.

As we walked down toward Nana's cabin, I spotted Alice outside on a rocking chair sipping on a steamy cup of coffee. She was watching a rusty cardinal who was perched silently upon the porch railing. As we got closer, the bird flew toward us, circled around our heads, then took off into the woods.

"You girls are up and at 'em extra early today!"

"You haven't seen a chicken walking around in blue overalls, have you?" Hope asked as if she was on some investigative television show.

"No, ma'am, but I do have a fresh loaf of banana bread ready to come out of the oven."

I suddenly perked up. "Oh! I want some!"

"Thought you might like a slice or two," Alice smiled as she walked us inside the aromatic cottage.

Aunt Esther was in the middle of eating a chunk *and* slicing off another piece. She guiltily looked at us with her mouth full and said, "You want a peiff?" I understood that she was actually offering us a piece, (and not a "peiff"). I nodded while holding my hands out, ready to stuff my cheeks. Hope couldn't resist the luscious, nutty, fortifying bread either.

"Here's some fresh milk that I got from Skwertz Dairy Farm."

Alice laughed. "You've got to be kiddin' me, right?"

"What?"

"Skwertz Dairy Farm?"

"Yeah?"

"Dairy squirts?" she emphasized. "When people are lactose intolerant, they usually have what is technically called the dairy squirts," Alice explained. "My kid brother was lactose intolerant, and many times he was stricken with the dairy squirts."

Aunt Esther shrugged and said, "You know, I never put that together, but now that I think about it, that is quite comical."

We all shared a good laugh.

"You know, that might be the first place we should go to find Noodle," Hope said. "Do they have chickens as well as cows?"

"Only one way to find out," Alice said.

"Okay then, Grace, are you ready?" Hope asked as she stood.

"Uh-huh!" I wiped my face then followed

Hope out of the door. That cardinal was back, right where she had been before. But she flew away when we closed the door.

Hope must really miss Noodle. She seemed so excited and determined to find him, I mean *her*. In fact, I had not seen her pick up one of her science books since we had been back from our trip.

My satisfied stomach and I walked along the country road. At the bottom of the hill was an old mill that went around and around as a trickling stream passed through. An emerald dragonfly was floating above the water getting a drink before it zoomed away. A couple of bulbous-looking blackberries were hiding in the bushes. When I looked closer, I saw an ample harvest waiting to be plucked. Even though I wasn't hungry, I couldn't resist the fresh fruit.

✑ *Ten* ✑

Ain't She Purdy?

The Skwertz's dairy farm was nestled in between two green pastures. We walked up the graveled road as Tater was proudly driving around a rather large red tractor. He looked too small to be driving such a serious machine.

Tater waved to us as we walked. He stopped, and shut off the tractor. "Hey there, y'all! How was y'alls campin' trip?" he asked as he climbed down.

"Aren't you a little young to be driving

that?" Hope asked.

"Shoot, no. I've been driving tractors since I was knee high to a grasshopper. My granddaddy taught me young. Want to go for a spin?" he offered.

Hope looked skeptical, as usual. "No … no. We're actually looking for Grace's chicken, Noodle," Hope said.

Tater's eyebrows scrunched like he wasn't exactly following what Hope was trying to say. "Huh?"

"When we were gone RVing, I lost my chicken, his, I mean, *her* name is Noodle and we were wondering if she may have come here to make friends with some other chickens," I clarified. "Do you have chickens?"

"Of course we have chickens! A farm ain't a real farm without chickens."

My face brightened.

"Y'all wanna go look in the coop? Maybe she's there?"

"Yes!" we both answered.

"Follow me," Tater signaled for us to hop over the fence. "Watch out for them cattle cookies. These ain't the kind you want to eat," he said as he pointed to mushy heaps of fly food, better known as *meadow muffins* or more commonly known as *cow dung*. One of the grazing cows decided to make a fresh pile of hot, smelly soft-serve right in front of us.

Yucko …

I wondered if cows were ever bashful about pooping so publicly. I was taught to do that kind of stuff in private.

Double Yucko …

We walked around a pond topped with blossoming lily pads next to a gigantic, green, drooping weeping willow tree. Within a large enclosed garden, Mr. Skwertz had constructed a ridiculously adorable garden shed. Tater opened the latch to this hidden delight. An archway of jasmine vines led us to the fanciest shed I had ever seen.

On either side of the pebbled pathway were raised boxes with all kinds of flowers and greens. Tripods of skinny cedar poles tied together at the tops provided bulbous tomato plants with something to climb. Another box was filled with pungent herbs like rosemary, parsley, sage, cloves, and mint.

I heard a buzzing sound coming from a tall stack of boxes. "What's that noise?" I asked.

"Honeybees, we give them plants to pollenate and the chickens eat the bugs that try to eat the plants then the bees thank the chickens by making us some delicious honey." Tater chuckled. "You should see it. My granddaddy puts on this big ole suit with a funny lookin' helmet, goes in there, and brings out big honeycombs, dripping with liquid gold."

"Wow! This is like a whole thriving symbiotic ecosystem," Hope said. "That's so cool."

Tater put his hand up to his mouth and spoke quietly. "Don't tell him I told you this, but my granddaddy built this for your nana. He built it hoping that your nana would marry him."

Hope and I didn't know what to say to that.

Tater went on. "Well, she definitely loved this garden but, sadly, not him."

Poor Mr. Skwertz. Even though I never thought about getting married, I imagined what it felt like to want someone to love you. My momma and papa were lucky because they both loved each other.

"There's the chicken coop right over there." Tater pointed to a giant wooden fancy painted dollhouse.

If I was a chicken, I would definitely want

to live in this fancy pink, white and yellow scalloped hen house. Tater pulled down a little window that opened to a light-brown, very surprised clucking chicken perched in a nest. "This your chicken?"

"Nope." I knew right away that this was not Noodle.

As he closed the window, he said, "Come around here and you can get a good look at them all." Tater opened the side door for us to go inside. Wood chips carpeted every surface. It was like a small scaled egg-laying factory. These must be some happy chickens because they laid a ton of white, brown, and blue speckled eggs. Attached to the one side was a wired chicken run for the chickens to eat bugs and other pests that try to destroy the garden, at least that's what Tater had explained.

I put my eyes on every little chicken, but, sadly, none of them were my Noodle. The door creaked open, and Mr. Skwertz peeked inside. "Well, howdy do! I wasn't expecting to see such *purdy* new hens in my hen house," Mr. Skwertz said with a smirk. "Y'all need some eggs?" He held up a basket for us to use.

"They're here looking for their lost chicken," Tater said.

"Oh, well, uh …" Mr. Skwertz scratched his head. "I haven't seen any new chickens 'round here. I know each and every one of *my* ladies by name." A smile snuck up on his face. "See, that's Violet. Over there is Ruby. But here's my favorite, Petunia … Ain't she purdy?" He held up a fat fluffy white chicken who flapped her wings trying to get away. "Now, don't you play hard to get," he said in a tone that people used when speaking to babies or pets they adored. "I know, I know … they're just visitin' … now you be nice … I love you, too, Petunia." He kissed the now calm chicken. "Ain't she so purdy?" he asked again.

"Oh, yes," we said. Obviously Mr. Skwertz loved his "purdy" chicken. It was funny watching him nuzzle her. She seemed to like it too after she had calmed down. We laughed as we watched Petunia pecking at the seeds Mr. Skwertz pulled from his pocket.

After Mr. Skwertz insisted on giving us a basket of fresh eggs, we went back on our search for Noodle. The sun was high in the sky as white puffy clouds floated around racing through one another.

"Want me to carry the basket?" Hope asked as I kept switching the heavy eggs from arm to arm.

"I got it," I said, acting independent.

"Just give it to me for a while then we'll switch back," Hope offered. That was a great idea I thought, so I handed the egg-filled basket over to Hope.

ᴄᴏ *Eleven* ᴏᴠ

The Force

We came to the next farm but what had greeted us was not friendly like Tater happily riding around on a giant tractor. A ferocious, barking German Shepherd wanted to kill us for even thinking about walking past his fence. His jaws snapped open and shut with each ear-piercing bark. His ears laid back and his tail stood tall while he seemed to wet himself each time he barked.

Everything in his body language told us

to beware. I'd never heard a louder or more terrifying bark. Hope and I ran as quickly as possible to get away from this dreadful monster. The dog chased us until it came to the end of the corner of a chain-linked fence. The crooked sign reading "Beware of Dog" that was meant to warn passersby was a terrible understatement. This dog was a killer.

Out of breath and beyond the dog's sight, Hope and I finally took a break.

"Poop," she said.

"What?"

"I dropped some eggs." She looked back at the trail of cracked eggs spilling out their yellow yolks along the black asphalt.

"Oopsies daisies," I said. That wasn't good. All those poor eggs now ruined, thanks to that despicable monster. "We still have some, right?" After seeing Hope's disappointment, I tried to offer a solution. "I think we should call it a day. It has to be past lunch, and I don't know about you, but I'm starving."

"But, we haven't found Noodle yet," Hope said in a strange way.

That was true … So far, not so good … we had just broken a bunch of perfectly great eggs, and we were still Noodle-less. But, I couldn't ignore the strange feeling I had. Why did Hope care so much about finding Noodle? "Hope, I get the feeling that there is some other thing you are looking for … *or maybe*, trying to get away from."

Hope looked down then shook her head. "For a dumb kid, you are pretty smart … sometimes."

I wasn't sure how to take that insult-filled compliment. "Uh …"

Hope looked up then exhaled. "I'm actually trying to avoid Papa."

"Papa?" I would never want to avoid Papa! He always made me feel extra loved. "Why?"

"Because he wants to talk to me about the birds and the bees." Hope seemed upset by this.

"The birds and the bees?" I thought about the chickens and the honeybees back at Mr. Skwertz's dairy farm. What was it about them that Hope didn't want to know?

"I already know about the birds and the bees, and I don't want to talk about it with Papa."

"Oh," I said. I guess we already did know what we needed to know about the birds and the bees because Tater did a pretty darn good job explaining how the bees made honey and how the chickens ate up the pests that might try to eat the plants. And if there were no plants, what would the bees eat in order to make the honey? So yeah, what was Papa wanting to tell Hope that we didn't already know? "Just tell him that Tater Skwertz showed us everything we would ever need to know about the birds and the bees already!" I had come up with the perfect plan!

Hope rolled her eyes. "I changed my mind … you are dumb."

"Huh?" I was confused … *not dumb*. Or was I? I didn't know which because I was too confused to know if I was dumb or not!

"I really don't want to walk past that dog again," Hope said as she set down the basket of eggs to tie her shoes.

"Me, neither."

From around the bend, I heard a strange sounding set of motors as two kids riding on bikes rode toward us. I slowly made out the two familiar forms of Smith and Wesson Springfield.

"Hi! Smith. Hi! Wesson," I said as they pedaled up to us.

"What are y'all doing up here at The Junkins' Farm?"

I couldn't believe my ears. "Did you say Junkins?"

"Yeah, look at the mailbox," Smith said.

I turned to see a crooked, old, rusty mailbox with faded letters that spelled out: JUNKI S. The "N" was missing but I could still see the shadow of where it had been. I wondered if this was the same Judd Junkins that Mr. Box had told me about.

"You know the Junkins?" I asked.

"Not really. Our daddy does though," Wesson said.

"Their dog is ugly and mean," Hope said.

"That old dog is all bark and no bite," Smith said.

"I doubt that," Hope retorted.

"You scared of old Pisser?" Wesson acted like it was such a crazy notion to be frightened by that ferocious beast.

"Pisser? Is that the dog's name? That's terrible." Hope shook her head.

"If you had a name like Pisser, wouldn't you be a jerk, too?" Smith said.

I sure was glad Momma didn't name me Pisser. I thought back to what Mr. Box had said about names and how they said a lot about a person ... and dogs ... namely Mr. Box's dog,

Stinky, who was very smelly.

"C'mon girls, follow us. Pisser don't bark at us. He's too skerd," Wesson said.

Hope flashed her usual skeptical look before she went to pick up the egg basket, but I grabbed it before she could. "I got it."

She smiled and said, "Thank you, Grace."

As we walked, and Smith and Wesson rode past the Junkins' farm, there was complete silence except for their "motors", some crickets, and other insects who chirped or whistled within the grass. Pisser just sat, panting as if we weren't even there. Smith and Wesson were right; Pisser didn't bark at them or us. It was as if they had some kind of power over the dog.

"How did you do that?" I asked after we got past the fence.

"The force is strong with us."

"Huh?" Hope said.

"Oh! I know, you're talking about Luke and Han," I said remembering that they had named their bikes after two *Star Wars* characters.

"Obviously you must put up some kind of force field because that dog was totally different when we passed," Hope concluded from the puzzling quandary.

"Like we said, the force," Smith said.

"Y'all wanna come over and meet our new chicken?" Wesson asked.

ঙ *Twelve* ઌ

The Egg Layer

"New chicken?" I gasped.

"Yeah, a couple weeks ago she wandered up wearing a certain blue pair of overalls," Wesson explained in a hinting manner.

"Noodle!" I jumped up excitedly as all of the remaining eggs bounced out of the basket, breaking on the ground.

Hope gave me a look that said, *See, you are dumb.*

I didn't care about the eggs. We found

Noodle! "Let's go!!!!" I kept leaping in the air as we skipped, jumped, and ran toward the Springfield's farm.

"You look like a kangaroo," Hope said with a slight smile on her face.

"I don't care what I look like, I'm just so happy!"

My stomach was gurgling, but I tried to ignore it as we got to their gate. Most of the time, Smith and Wesson played over near my house. I had been here plenty times before, but usually with Momma because Smith and Wesson's mother was friends with mine.

They lived in a sprawling white farmhouse topped with a silver tin roof. "Spring Fever Farm" was loaded with lots of goats, donkeys, horses, cows, ducks, swans, chickens, and you name it. My favorite sound was hearing the donkeys "heehaw" to Smith and Wesson as they passed. I circled back to the donkeys and let their soft fuzzy lips tickle my palm before I pet in between their long wiggly ears. Donkeys have the sweetest eyes, I decided, as I stared into their reflective brown orbs.

A jealous pink pig walked up and snorted, asking for a snack, but I didn't have anything to share. "Sorry, Piggy, I know how you feel.

I'm hungry, too." The animals had their own corrals, but a lot of them wandered around into the other animal's pens.

The stream that went by our house also curved around the Springfield's. Horses grazed along the rolling green pastures while black and white cows sipped from a sparkling pond. In the middle of the large pond was an island with a tall tree that shaded the whole center, providing a tranquil place for the ducks and swans to swim.

If I was a lonely chicken, I might find this place to be just right. "Where's Noodle?" I asked.

"She's over in the hen house, laying eggs with all the other chickens," Wesson said as they led us over to the barnyard.

"Laying eggs?"

"Yep," Smith said casually.

"I gotta see this," I said.

"Well, what did you think a chicken would do?" Hope asked as if she always knew Noodle would be a momma.

"I don't know? I never owned a chicken before," I said while shrugging my shoulders with my hands up in the air.

As we walked into the chicken coop, my

eyes took a second to adjust to the dimmer light. Feathers flew around as the chickens strutted to and fro. A couple of laying hens got up after their eggs were dropped within the nests.

I looked around but none of the chickens were dressed in any special kind of apparel. "Which one is Noodle?"

"Can't you tell?" Hope asked.

"No, they look all the same," I said.

"Not this one," Smith said from behind. He was holding a chicken that was in a red, yellow, and white dress.

"Noodle!" She looked so fancy, but I would know my Noodle in any kind of apparel. I grabbed her and gave her a big hug. She didn't pull away like Petunia had in Mr. Skwertz's arms. She let me hug her right away. "Where did you find this dress?"

"Well, we figured since she was laying eggs, she might want something a little more suitable for such a job," Wesson explained. "So our momma sewed her this one since those overalls were getting in the way of her eggs dropping into the nest."

"Aww! It looks so good on her!"

Hope reluctantly agreed, "It really does suit her nicely."

Maybe Hope really did care about Noodle, after all.

"Our momma knew how this chicken liked to wear the latest and greatest Grace Newton fashions," Smith joked.

"So Noodle lays eggs?" I asked.

"Yeah, around six months old, chickens start laying eggs."

I did the math. Yup, Noodle was a little over six months old. "Have any of them hatched?"

"No, they aren't fertilized."

"How do they get fertilized?" I asked.

Hope cleared her throat and said, "Next subject."

ஃ *Thirteen* ஃ

Egg Salad and Matching Dresses

Mrs. Springfield walked into the coop wearing a dress that matched Noodle's. She must have made a miniature version for Noodle.

"Hello Mrs. Springfield," Hope greeted.

"You look beautiful, Mrs. Springfield!" I couldn't help but utter.

Mrs. Springfield blushed, throwing her hands down, being ever so modest. "Now you youngins know better! Y'all call me Miss Josie, remember?"

"Yes, Miss Josie," we politely answered.

"Y'all hungry? I was just about to make some egg salad sandwiches for Smith and Wesson."

I don't think I could have ever been hungrier in all of my life! I wanted to eat like sixteen hundred thousand egg salad sandwiches right about now.

"I was just gathering a dozen or so eggs to make a fresh batch," she said as she was putting eggs, one by one, into a basket similar to the one Mr. Skwertz used to gather the eggs that we had just accidentally broken and scattered all over the road near the Junkins' farm. It wasn't our fault. It was that Pisser's fault, I silently blamed that ferocious girl-eating dog.

We walked inside the Springfield's kitchen. All I could see were a bunch of animal heads displayed from every wall around the whole house. Mr. Springfield was a big time hunter. He loved going out for weeks at a time bringing home big game for his family to eat for months. It was up to Mrs. Springfield and the older kids to manage the farm, animals, and garden when he was gone. Mr. Springfield did most of the heavy-lifting part of farming, but when that was all squared away, he was hunting.

I looked out at the Springfield's vegetable garden. It was very similar to ours—the one that Momma spent a lot of time in. It was very nice and produced some healthy vegetables. In fact, most everyone in Apple Valley seemed to have their own vegetable garden, but I have to say, Mr. Skwertz had the loveliest, most orderly garden I had ever seen.

Miss Josie got out a pot steamer and placed the dozen or so eggs within the basket then turned on the old-fashioned gas stove. Those eggs couldn't cook quick enough as far as I was concerned.

A thick pineapple-shaped cutting board held a fresh-baked loaf of seeded bread that Miss Josie cut a few slices from.

As we sat at the table, holding our scrumptious egg salad sandwiches, I looked around her cheerful kitchen. Our mouths were smacking as we ate. It was a weird, kind of yucky sound ... eating. Smith and Wesson had two older sisters, Dolly and Sissy, but they were in high school so I barely got to see them. I guess Hope was thinking the same thing I was because she asked about what I was wondering.

"Where are Sissy and Dolly?" Hope asked Miss Josie.

"They're at cheerleading camp over in Beaumont. They'll be back at the end of the week."

Smith and Wesson stood up and pretended to cheer saying, "Give me a D, give me a U, give me an M, give me a B. What's that spell?"

When I arranged all those letters into a word inside my head, it didn't make sense.

Hope snickered, but Miss Josie said, "Y'all quit it! That's not nice. Your sisters love cheerleadin', and they are darn good, if I say so myself. And they ain't afraid to go huntin' with their daddy like some kids I know."

That shut Smith and Wesson right up. I could see those words were hard to swallow because they were struggling with their sandwiches suddenly.

"So are you going to bring Noodle home with us?" Hope asked.

I hadn't thought that there was any other option. Of course Noodle was coming home with us! But then again, was I being selfish? It didn't matter, because she was my chicken, so that solved that dilemma.

"Yes, of course!" I said.

After Miss Josie sent us away with a few more dresses for Noodle to wear, we walked back home. Noodle snuggled into my forearm as I held her. I smiled as I watched her little neck bob with each one of my steps. She did look so much more girly in her dress. I felt her stomach clench as she let out a cluck, then something warm popped and an egg appeared. It landed in my other hand. Boy, was I glad it wasn't poop. I held it up to Hope who smiled as she shook her head in disbelief.

"At least we won't be coming home empty-handed," she said.

AMAZING GRACE NEWTON

ເ∕ Fourteen ∂ເ

Poor Aunt Esther

As we were walking back up the hill, I heard an awful coughing fit coming from Nana's cottage. The same cardinal was still perched on the railing.

"That doesn't sound good," Hope said.

"Should we go see?"

"Yeah, probably," she said as she hopped up the stairs.

The coughing fit began again. It sounded even more horrible the closer we got.

"Knock, knock," Hope said as we gently opened the door.

Aunt Esther was lying on the couch covered by a red plaid blanket and a skinny glass thermometer sticking out of her mouth. Alice was standing next to her getting ready to read her temperature.

"Oh, no! Are you sick?" I asked.

"'Fraid so, you might not want to get too close. It could be a flu," Alice warned.

"But she was fine this morning!" Hope said.

"It's probably nothing," Aunt Esther said before coughing again. "Probably just the dust from all the cleaning yesterday. I'll be better soon, I'm sure," she said while trying to reassure us with a smile.

Poor Aunt Esther! I didn't like seeing her like this. She was always full of calm energy. She wasn't super active but she also never sat around.

"Oh, you found Noodle!" she exclaimed.

"Well, now that is a relief!" Alice said while walking over to give Noodle a gentle caress. "Isn't she adorable in that dress? Where did you find her?"

"She was over at Smith and Wesson Springfield's farm making friends and dropping eggs. Look, she dropped one just now," I exclaimed as I showed them her fresh big brown egg.

"Well, I'll be darned. How is Josie?" Aunt Esther asked.

"Great, she said she was going to come over and visit real soon. She said it had been too long. I told her you were here, too," I said.

"Hopefully, I'll be all better before she comes," Aunt Esther said as a coughing fit took over, causing Noodle to nervously cluck and want to jump out of my grip.

"We better get Noodle home before she runs away, again," Hope said.

"Okay, well, I hope you feel better soon, Aunt Esther," I said.

"I will. I'll feel better soon, I promise."

AMAZING GRACE NEWTON

✍ *Fifteen* ✍

Show and Tell

Momma and Papa were so excited that we had found Noodle. As soon as Hope and I got home, we spent the next few minutes telling them all about our day. I watched as Hope tried to stay clear of Papa. I wanted to make this silly situation all better as soon as possible. So, in exchange for helping me find Noodle, I decided to do Hope a favor and tell Papa that he no longer needed to explain the birds and the bees to Hope *or* to me.

"Oh, yeah?" he gave me a challenging look.

"Yeah."

"How's that?"

"Because, Tater Skwertz showed us everything about how the birds and the bees work. He did a real good job explaining everything and even how to ..."

Papa cut me off and grabbed me by the shoulders. "He did what?" Papa's usual look of love that was reserved for us was gone. I hadn't ever seen this look in his eyes before. Momma stood holding her heart, with worry smeared all over her face.

Before I could explain more, Papa released my shoulders, bolted outside and took off in his pickup truck.

"Great, why did you have to do that?" Hope looked so angry with me. "After all I've done for you!"

Here I thought I was doing something good, but it seemed to make everyone angry.

"Grace, what exactly did Tater show and tell you?" Momma calmly asked.

Hope chimed in, "It's *sooooo* not what you're thinking. He literally showed us his grandfather's herb garden that has honeybees and chickens."

Hope wasn't detailing the story quite right so I butted in. "The chickens eat the bugs that eat the plants, then the chickens poop the fertilizer that makes the plants grow fuller. The bees pollenate the flowers then make liquid gold," I explained as Momma's relief returned to her features.

But then the panic appeared when she said, "We have to warm Mr. Skwertz that Papa is on his way over to kill Tater."

"Why would he want to kill Tater?" I wondered as Momma picked up the phone to call Mr. Skwertz. After ten rings, no one answered.

"What if we're too late?" Hope asked.

"We have to go find him before he does something we'll all regret," Momma said.

"But Papa has the truck," I said.

"We'll have to go on foot. Hope, you stay here with Abel," Momma said as Abel came running into the room.

"Noodle!" Abel exclaimed as he saw my chicken.

"No, I'm going too. I have to explain this to Papa," Hope said.

"Well, we might already be too late. No time to argue, Abel you're just going to have to come with us. Can you keep up?" Momma asked a silly question, I thought. Of course, Abel could keep up *and* outrun us all.

I ran and put Noodle in the mudroom before catching up to everyone in the driveway.

• • •

Fall was whispering its arrival in the late August air. I wanted to run over to Mazie and tell her that I had found Noodle, but we were in too much of a hurry.

I watched everyone getting into Aunt Esther's Jeep. *That was a good idea*, I thought. We would get there much faster by car. Hope held her arm up to help me climb in as Momma started the engine.

"Oh, it's been so long since I've driven a stick," Momma nervously said. She pushed down the clutch then ground the gears into reverse. The engine stalled.

"Heck!" Momma said. "Okay, I got this," she told herself as she restarted the engine. This time she barely ground the gears and even was able to back up. Carefully, she got the hang of it. Then she took off like a bullet train headed straight for the Skwertz.

When we got to the dairy farm, Papa was banging on the front door of the main house. We watched as Mr. Skwertz and Tater cheerfully opened the door.

"Papa! Papa!" I called. He turned his back to us and walked inside the old man's house holding Tater's neck.

Hope jumped out. "Papa! Papa!!! It's not what you think!" she screamed.

We all ran up to the house to hear Mr. Skwertz saying, "Now, you just hold on one minute. What in tarnation is going on around here?"

"You know what my daughter's just told me?" Papa said. "Your grandson … this here guy, showed them all about the birds and the bees," Papa's eyes were so red with rage, I thought poor Tater's head was going to pop off under his grip.

Mr. Skwertz looked confused as he tried to make sense of what my papa was saying. Tater was so terrified that he wouldn't say a word.

"Papa, you need to listen to me right now," Hope said.

"Papa, please!" I plead.

"Lumin, let the boy's neck go," Momma said.

Papa released his grip then turned his eyes over to Hope.

"Tater, could you please show Papa the garden where you have birds also known as chickens and bees that make honey?" Hope said in a manner more suitable for an adult.

Papa looked confused now. "What are you talking about?"

"C'mon, we'll *show* you," Hope said as she led everyone out to the garden without neglecting to give me a certain look of irritation.

The garden was beautiful during the day but it was extra special at night. Mr. Skwertz had the trees, vines, and bushes magically lit with twinkly white lights. It was a shame that we were coming here under such harsh circumstances.

Hope explained everything because obviously I had made a mess with my attempt to recount our day. "When we were looking for Noodle, we came here, and Tater showed us around this impressive ecosystem that uses birds and bees to produce flowers, herbs, vegetables, and honey. Grace misunderstood when I told her that you wanted to talk to me about the same subject, and she tried to reassure you by saying that Tater had explained all that we needed to know about the birds and the bees."

Papa wiped his hand over his shameful face, leaving it in a rather sheepish expression. I could tell that he felt bad for handling Tater so roughly. Tater rubbed his neck, either trying to get the feeling back or trying to make what hurt feel better. *Poor guy*, I thought.

Papa cleared his throat. "Tater, Mr. Skwertz, I owe you all an apology. And not only that, but I will make it up to you … somehow. I truly am sorry for jumping to such an unspeakable conclusion."

"Lumin, I know raising daughters is a tough job. Believe me, Tater's mother had me worried sick, and rightfully so, but let me tell ya, Tater here, is a real gentleman." Mr. Skwertz put his arm around his grandson as tears puddled in the bottoms of his eyes. "And I am real proud of him." He sniffed. Mr. Skwertz's emotions were contagious as he tearfully spoke. "I would bet my whole farm that he would never do anything to spoil the hard work y'all are doing in raising a fine family."

Papa got down on his knee and looked directly into Tater's big blue eyes. "Son, I owe you a special apology. I am terribly sorry for putting my hands on you in anger. Your granddaddy is right; I can tell that you are a fine young man, and I should have used my better judgment." Papa extended his hand for shaking, but, Tater, forgivingly, offered him a hug.

In a matter of seconds it turned into a group hug. Tears flowed as forgiveness was granted under a beautifully arched jasmine walkway, lit with twinkly white lights.

AND THE MISSING NOODLE

∽ Sixteen ∽

Rainbow Farts

That was a long day, I thought as I was lying in bed. A fresh, gentle breeze rolled over my body from outside of my bedroom window. I looked at my hands. I had some dirt under my fingernails that I tried to scoop out.

Papa stood at my door and said, "Hey there, little darlin'. You mad at me?"

I looked up and smiled. "Hi, Papa. Why would I be mad at you?"

"For losing my temper with Tater. Poor

little guy. I should have waited before assuming the worst." Papa was beating himself up; I could tell.

"It's okay, Papa," I said sadly.

Papa examined my face. "Is everything okay with you?" he asked.

Guess I looked sad or something. "Oh, nothing really ... I'm just thinking about a lot of stuff."

"Like what?"

"Well, I was thinking about Aunt Esther."

"What about Aunt Esther?"

I remembered that no one but I knew that she had cancer. So, I couldn't tell him about that, but now that I opened my mouth, I had to say something. "It's just that I don't like seeing her sick."

"She's sick?"

"She said it's just from the dust, but I don't want her to die," I said with a little extra unplanned despair.

Papa laughed but not in a funny way. "Darlin', I have never heard of someone dying from dust."

"But what if she does die?" I asked, hoping he would say some words that could make me feel better.

"She won't. I promise."

"How do you know?"

"I have faith."

"What's that?"

"Faith is believing in something when you can't see it."

"Oh."

"So, Aunt Esther may look to be sick right now, but if you have faith and pray, she will get better."

How could Papa be so sure? He didn't know what I knew.

He must have been reading my doubtful mind. "You know how you were wishing on those shooting stars?" he asked.

"Yes."

"Well, you had to have faith knowing that when you wished, it would come true."

"But what if you wish for something that can't ever come true?"

"If you have faith, anything is possible." Papa gave me a kiss on my forehead then said, "Guess what?"

"What?"

"I'm so excited for you," he said with his expression matching his sentence.

I had no idea why he would be excited.

"Why?"

"Because you're about to go to the most fantastic place in the whole world!" His eyes bulged.

My eyes bulged too, reflecting his face. "Where?"

"Dreamland! Where you can run over rainbows, sleep inside cloud castles, and dance with unicorns that fart rainbows!"

I giggled at that and, also, because he tickled my neck.

"Plus, you can float around inside bubbles and swim underwater without needing to come up for air!"

Wow! I thought. I couldn't wait to go to Dreamland!

"Sweet dreams," Papa said as he switched off the light.

"Sweet dreams," I said back.

My brain was still overactive. It was spinning, thinking about the day. Before I could settle down, for some reason, I felt the need to pray. I slid off the side of my bed and kneeled. I put my hands together and thanked God for a lot of things like Papa not killing Tater, for helping me find Noodle, and for giving me a comfortable bed to sleep in. But most importantly, I prayed that Aunt Esther would feel better and that Hope wouldn't still be mad at me as she seemed to still be holding a small grudge. I climbed back up into bed and with the sweet breezes, drifted off to sleep.

If I went to Dreamland, I couldn't remember when I woke up in the morning. I jumped down ready to greet Noodle at breakfast. I went to open the door to the mudroom but it was already opened. I peeked inside and found an egg on top of a pile of dirty laundry but no Noodle. I walked into the kitchen and asked Momma if she had seen Noodle.

"She's probably in the garden nibbling on some grubs," Momma said as she was flipping some french toast.

I walked outside, careful to not slam the screen door but I couldn't find Noodle. I did find Mazie though.

"Hi! Mazie!" I greeted.

"Hi!"

"I'm looking for Noodle, again."

"Again?"

"Yes, we found him, I mean *her*, over at Smith and Wesson's house yesterday but I can't find her this morning."

"Did you look in the barn?" she asked.

111

"No, but I will right now. I'll be right back."

I ran over to the barn and slid open the giant heavy door. All that was in there was old farming equipment, tractors, tools, and Princess Leia, my bicycle. She looked like she was waiting for me. I swung my leg over and took Leia for a spin. I took a couple of spins then rode back over to my puddle.

"She's not in the barn, but I did find my bike!"

"I see that!"

"Yeah," I sort of showed off by trying to do some wheelies.

"Grace, breakfast is ready," Momma called.

◈ *Seventeen* ◈

It Pooped

Even though Momma's call got my attention, the irresistible toasty aroma alone summoned me into the kitchen. I sat down, holding my fork and knife up in the air ready to attack my food. "Put your silverware down, honey. You're not an animal, are you?"

Come to think of it, I had never seen an animal use any kind of silverware, properly, or at all. "No," I said as I let my arms down. "Just ferociously hungry."

Momma snickered. "Okay, here ya go," Momma said as she set down a stack of three golden browned pieces of french toast, dripping with a scoop of Momma's homemade soft butter and sweet maple syrup.

Abel zoomed in holding Noodle in his outstretched arms.

"Noodle!" I joyfully exclaimed as Abel zoomed past me. "Where did you find her?"

Abel set her down in the mudroom where I had put her last. "Found her trying to escape," he said from down the hall. "She was on her way back to the neighbor's farm."

Momma gave me a look, expressing concern with her eyebrows.

Hmmmm. I wondered what that meant, her look and the fact that Noodle was trying to escape?

I took a big bite of breakfast, pondering what this could mean. Abel looked into the mudroom where he had left Noodle before he came to sit next to me with his breakfast.

"It pooped," he said as he sat accidentally knocking his fork to the floor. "Oops."

"What?" I almost accidentally knocked my whole plate over. "Whoa! That was close." I was relieved that I caught it before it dropped but almost forgot what we were talking about. "What?"

"Noodle pooped," he said as he casually nibbled on his breakfast.

"Huh? Where?"

"In the laundry basket."

"That's an egg," I explained.

"I think it pooped, too." He shrugged.

Momma went to look. After a minute, I heard her start a load of laundry. As she walked back into the kitchen, she said, "I think Noodle needs to stay outside, Grace. Chickens are really outdoor pets."

"But!" I said with my mouth stuffed.

"No buts. Abel, put Noodle out," Momma closed the argument.

Poop.

All I really wanted to say was "but" but Momma said that I couldn't say "but" so I said, "What if she runs away again?"

"Why don't you and your father build her a proper chicken coop like you see at the Springfield's or the Skwertz'?"

My head tilted, imagining the construction. That wasn't a bad idea!

The phone rang. Momma picked it up and said, "Hello? ... Who's speaking? Uh-huh ..."

She held the receiver to her chest then yelled, "Hope!" Momma called upstairs, "Telephone is for you, *and* it's time for breakfast."

"Who's that?" I asked.

Momma shrugged.

"Where's Papa?" I asked another question.

"He's over at the Skwertz' farm, working off his guilt."

"What's he doing?" I just knew Momma was about to say, *What, is this twenty questions or what?* But she didn't.

"Milking the cows, I'd imagine."

Hope came down then took the phone into the other room. I heard her quietly say, "Hello?"

"I wonder where Esther and Alice are this morning?" Momma asked.

"Hopefully Aunt Esther is feeling better; I prayed for her last night," I said.

Momma turned to me. "She's sick?"

"Yeah, she said it's from all the dust, though."

"Oh, well then, I'll just bring them over a plate of food."

"I'll come, too!" I said, stuffing the last piece of toast into my mouth.

AND THE MISSING NOODLE

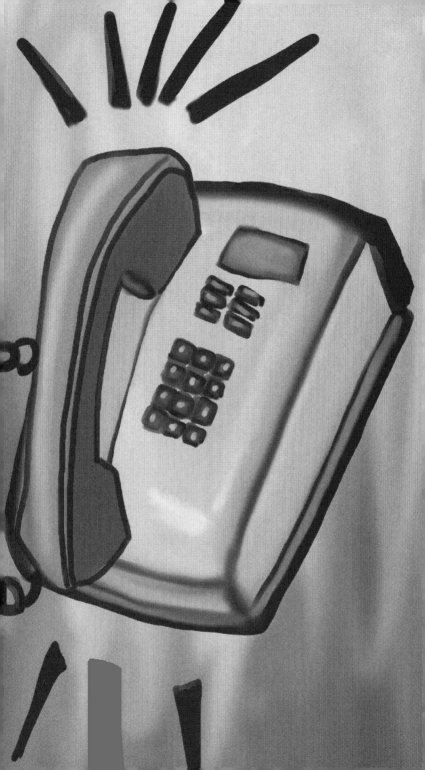

❧ Eighteen ❧
Who's Calling?

"Hello stranger!" Hope heard a boy's voice say.

"Stefan!" Hope said but then covered her mouth in order to not draw too much attention from her papa or anyone else who might be listening.

"How's life on the farm?" he asked.

"Same as always. Are you home yet?"

"Yeah, we're home. It's boring … you know." He was quiet for a minute and Hope didn't know what to say either but then he spoke, "I miss you."

Hope blushed while twirling her hair around her fingers. She sat down on the floor and felt little butterflies fluttering around, inside her gut.

"Do you miss me?" Stefan asked.

Reluctantly, Hope said, "Yes."

"I knew it!" This seemed to make Stefan happy although Hope couldn't quite understand how missing someone should make another person happy. All these strange feelings made Hope wish that growing up wasn't so inner-sensory. She wasn't sure if inner-sensory was a real word but it precisely summed up what she was feeling.

"So, how are the driving lessons coming along?" Hope asked.

"I should be ready to come visit you very soon."

Hope was confused. That wasn't the question she had asked, but maybe he had jumped right to the point of his call.

"Oh yeah? When?"

"Maybe, right before school starts?"

Hope envisioned Stefan arriving at their home. She imagined the look on her Papa's face last night. Then she imagined those two scenes together—Stefan and her papa. "Actually, my papa has been acting a little strange because Grace accidentally told him that I met a boy, *you*, and then she said that another boy told us all about the birds and the bees. So, I'm not sure that it would be the best time for you to come visit just now. Maybe when my papa cools down a bit."

Stefan's voice went from playful to concern. "What boy told you about the birds and the bees?"

"No, it's not what you think, but it's a long story."

"I got time."

Hope replayed the whole miscommunication to Stefan who laughed extra hard at poor Tater who almost had his head popped off.

"Ahhhh … that *is* funny stuff. That'll teach a guy to bring two lassies on a tour of his chicken coop."

"I guess," Hope agreed. "But I still feel bad for Tater. He's young! … Like maybe a year or two older than Grace. And you haven't met my papa. You'd be scared, too."

"I, for one, hope I never do anything to

make your papa mad." Stefan got a chill that Hope could feel hundreds of miles away.

AND THE MISSING NOODLE

◌ Nineteen ◌

Midnight Magic

When we got to Nana's cottage, Aunt Esther looked worse than the day before. She was coughing and looked like she was in pain. Was this what cancer looked like? Oh no! What if Aunt Esther died like Nana?

Momma set down the plate and rushed over to her sister's side. She placed her hands on Aunt Esther's forehead then touched her cheeks—the very same way she touched us kids when we were sick. Momma looked concerned.

"I think we should take you to go see a doctor," Momma said.

Alice nodded her head in agreement, but Aunt Esther said, "No, no, I'll be fine. It's just a little cold. I'll be better in a couple days."

Momma didn't look convinced as she took Aunt Esther's hand and placed it within her own. "Well, then, I think I better make you some tea."

"I gave her some tea this morning but there it is, untouched." With worry written all over her face, Alice gestured to the side table.

"Oh, um … not that kind of tea. I will make her the special tea that our momma gave to us when we were sick. Hopefully that will help." Momma's face turned from worry to determination.

"Oh, okay." Alice shrugged.

"C'mon, Grace, we need to go to the garden."

I followed, ready to do whatever it took to help Aunt Esther.

Momma picked, plucked, peeled, ground, then steeped a concoction with which I was very familiar. As she was preparing her miracle drink, she explained what each item was and why she was using it.

"Okay, Grace, pay attention just in case you need to make this one day for your children."

"Yes, Momma," I said.

"I'm chopping up some garlic for its anti-viral, antibiotic, and antiseptic properties." Whatever that meant, I assumed was good even though it sounded anti-good. "Onion, of course, is for the cough. It helps to keep the respiratory tract open." That sounded sort of better. She threw the diced onion into the pot then picked up a weird root-looking thing. "Ginger will calm her stomach while sage will ease her sore throat." That was definitely good, I thought. "Thyme will bring whatever it is that's making her cough, out, but here's the real kicker ... Cayenne pepper will actually kick the flu or cold or whatever it is right out of her." I smiled knowing this red powder was going to fight for Aunt Esther when she was weak. "You can never ever have too much honey, honey," she gave me a loving look that made me blush as she drizzled a bunch of liquid gold into the potion. "And last but not least, lemon. Lemon is loaded with vitamin C and it will overpower whatever it is that has got a hold on her."

Anytime we kids came down with anything, Momma made this same herbal tea. It tasted so horrible that we refused to get sick ... just so we wouldn't have to drink that reddish, tar-tasting rubbish. Momma called it "midnight magic" but we called it "wicked witch's blood".

We brought our potion back down to the cabin. Aunt Esther knew fighting Momma was useless so she voluntarily drank the elixir. Momma quietly said as she drank, "A cup of midnight magic makes everything better." Aunt Esther proceeded to fall into a healing sleep for the rest of the afternoon.

৵ *Twenty* ৵

The Bet

Mr. Skwertz gave my Papa a few more young chicks for Noodle to mother and also to hang around with because he said that my father had not only repaid his debt but was now over doing it. In addition, he helped my Papa plan a similar version of the fantastic ecosystem that they had over at the Skwertz' farm.

Noodle and her friends, that we had yet to name, were so much happier clucking the days away together. But that didn't keep Noodle from trying and successfully escaping back over to the Springfield's farm.

I woke up one morning and couldn't find Noodle anywhere. But when I rode my bike over to the Springfield's farm, I saw Smith and Wesson playing a game of fetch with her.

"Hey!" I cried. "What are you doing over here?" I asked Noodle.

"Guess she just misses playing our games," Wesson said.

"Did you teach her how to play fetch?" I asked.

"That and soccer, too. Look!" they said as they kicked a light little bouncy ball over to her and she hit it back with her head.

"Well, I have seen it all," I breathlessly exclaimed.

"Wanna play, too?" Smith asked.

"Yeah!" I said as I gently kicked the ball back to Noodle who returned it once again with her head. I knew Noodle was special, but I never knew how much.

We played various games with Noodle until she got tired and it was time for target practice.

"Y'all wanna make a bet that I can hit that can from way over here?" I said eyeing a can on top of the fence waiting to be shot down.

"You can't hit it from this far away. Even if you get on the mark, the stone'll drop before it even gets close enough."

"Wanna make a bet?" I challenged once again.

"I'll betcha," Smith said but then asked, "What are we bettin'?"

"How about we bet cleaning out the chicken coop for one week?" Wesson said.

"What do you mean?" I asked.

"If you miss, you have to clean out the chicken coop for one week."

"What if I get it?"

"You don't have to clean it out for one week."

"Hey! That's not fair!"

"Sure it is."

"Nuh-uh. How about if I get it, you two have to jump in the pond."

The twins looked at each other and then at the pond where all the animals either got their drinks or swam or who knows what else. It was certainly picturesque but not the kind of water that made you want to swim.

"Uh," Smith stalled.

"Well? Do we have a bet or not?"

"She ain't gonna make it anyways, might as

well say okay," Smith elbowed Wesson.

Wesson didn't seem as sure of my inability to hit the target as Smith. "Okay," he reluctantly agreed. "We have a bet."

I looked over in the distance and spotted my target. I closed my left eye to see if it moved at all. I closed my right eye, realizing that my right eye was much more accurate. I reached for the slingshot Smith had in his hands, slipped the rock into the sling, and took my position.

"She ain't never gonna hit that from here," Smith said under his breath.

I blocked out their chatter and brought the rubber-band back as far as it would allow. I lined up the can with the direction that the rock was going to make. I just had to keep the arch in mind. If I overshot it, the rock would go past it, yet if I didn't pull back enough, it wouldn't make it. I felt my arms getting weak as I held this position. It was time to shoot. I let go of the slingshot a little too late and the rock, very clumsily fell to the ground.

Poop. I wasn't even close.

Smith and Wesson crumbled to the ground in hysterics. Apparently my folly was their joy. I guess it was pretty funny watching the silly little rock plop to the ground. I laughed too until Smith and Wesson reminded me of what was at stake.

"Welcome to the staff here at Spring Fever Farm, here's your shovel and broom."

Double poop.

Eat, Pray, Grow...

Hope 9/15

Grace 9/15
Axel 9/15

Hope 8/13
Grace 8/13
Axel 8/13

Hope 10/13

Grace 10/13
Axel 10/13

ᓉ *Twenty-One* ᓉ
Growth Spurts

After a couple days of constant care from Momma and Alice, Aunt Esther began to feel better. It was right after Papa and I had finished Noodle's chicken coop and right before school was about to start.

I found Momma up in my room digging through the closet.

"Hi, Momma, you looking for something?"

"Yes, we need to make sure you have a couple of nice outfits to wear," Momma said.

"For what?"

"School is going to start in a couple of days."

"Aww, man!" I threw myself onto my bed. "Please, Momma, don't remind me," I said a little too dramatically.

"Too bad they don't have drama in the second grade because you would be the star student."

I had no idea what she was talking about; all I knew is that school stunk. "I don't want to go," I grumbled.

"C'mon Grace! You have to go to school, so you might as well look nice while you go," she said while holding up a too-small, older dress.

"No dresses," I said.

"But this one is so pretty on you," she said.

"I know, but it's school not church." I knew better than to look all fancy at school. The minute you stood out, kids loved to poke fun.

Momma agreed then looked through my pants, shorts, and shirts. "I think you may have outgrown almost everything," she said as she sifted through my clothes.

Abel walked in with the bottoms of his pants up above his ankles. "You, too?" she said when she looked at his pants. "I guess we should go shopping."

"My tooth is looth!" Abel exclaimed while wiggling around one of his bottom teeth.

"Huh?" I asked.

"Your tooth is loose?" Momma said. "Oh dear, you kids are growing up way too quickly for me!"

"Let me see!" I said.

Abel looked so excited as he showed me his moving tooth. "Grafe, it wav your wif! Wemember? The footing ftar?" Abel couldn't take his hands out of his mouth to talk. I guess he thought it would get tight again if he let it go.

"The shooting star?" I clarified. "Yes, I remember!"

Hope walked in with a pile of hand-me-downs. "Here, Grace, some of these might fit you, now."

"Oh!" I loved hand-me-downs. I jumped up and looked at all of Hope's used tactile treasures. We didn't exactly have the same style. When I say that, it means that I didn't really have any style. But Hope always looked so smart so it wouldn't hurt to look like her.

"What about me?" Abel asked after he finally stopped wiggling his tooth.

Momma thought for a minute. "Let's go

see what you have," she said as she rose and walked out of my room and into Abel's.

Hope stood there as I held up a couple of shirts to see if they would fit. "That one will look nice on you, especially for the first day of school."

"Oh … yeah …" I ruefully said.

"What's the matter?"

"School."

"Whatever, school is where you go to learn. Only ignorant people don't want to learn."

I did like to learn but just not there. It seemed that school was a place for other kids who wanted to make fun of me for not being as smart as them. I liked sewing or shooting my slingshot, doing stuff with my hands or going on vacation. School was boring, and none of the teachers I had had seemed to care about me. They liked the kids who were already smart.

"Whatever." Hope walked back out.

I stood, wishing that Hope would have stayed and talked to me for longer. Whenever she talked to me, I felt a little more important. I wondered if Abel felt the same way about me.

I went to see what Abel and Momma were doing but instead I felt led outside. I walked over to the old wishing well and looked down into the darkness. It seemed rather strange to make wishes in to something so empty or invisible. I guess that was what faith was, right? I recalled what Papa had told me about faith a couple of nights ago but I wasn't sure. Maybe Mazie would know.

The evening crickets were quietly chirping in the long grasses along the woodland. I kicked a pebble over to the puddle and peeked over.

"Hi, Mazie," I greeted.

"Hi, Grace, are you feeling down?"

How did Mazie always know how I was feeling? "Yes, a little."

"What is it?"

"School."

"What about it?"

"I don't want to go."

"Why not?"

"Because I'm not good at it."

"Just because you're not good at something doesn't mean you shouldn't try."

I must have looked confused.

Mazie asked, "Were you great at sewing the first time you tried?"

I remembered my first sewing experience. It went something like this: *Oopsies ... Ouchy ... Poopsies ...* "No."

"Then why would you be good at school right away? It takes time to learn. Remember, I will always be around to help you when you're feeling lost, even at school."

"Can you to go to school with me?"

"Wherever you go, I'll be there."

So far, what Mazie had said was true. When I was camping and got lost, Mazie or Mr. Box was there to help me. My mind wandered over to wondering how Mr. Box was doing? Was he still at Camp Igottapoopie with his new puppy? I thought about our awesome RV adventure and decided to go see how Aunt Esther was doing.

AND THE MISSING NOODLE

Twenty-Two

Momma Bear

Instead of the driveway, I went on the tippy toe trail through the woods. Maybe I would see that white magical deerie again. As I meandered, I picked up on an organic scent of decaying leaves mixed with pine needles. The trickling brook gently bubbled beside me. I saw some animal prints in the mud. I tried to figure out what this big fat wide claw was. When I put my skinny foot inside of it, there was plenty of room to spare. Whatever it was, was big.

Boy was I right. For some reason I knew I had to hide. Maybe it was the tingle that traveled down my spine. I ducked behind an old fallen tree that had a curtain of roots keeping it still alive in the earth. Dirt and other nesting materials were between the roots and the ground about three feet beneath it. I heard a grunting and a sniffing.

I was afraid to look, but what if it was just my overactive imagination and nothing at all? I'll tell you one thing, I never expected to see a black bear and three little cubs foraging for twigs, nuts, and berries. I froze. I wasn't sure what I should do so I ducked back down and hid behind the tree trunk. I heard the momma bear sniffing and snorting in my direction. Suddenly I had to go tinkle but I knew if she smelled that, I'd be in big trouble.

Nervous shaking spread all over my bones as I tried desperately to stay out of her sight. I thought about my options while hatching some sort of exit plan. I snuck a peek over the log and saw three black baby bears. They were so cute and cuddly-looking while they rolled around wrestling one another as the momma foraged, never letting down her guard. I was afraid to move. What if she saw me? I looked back at my house … it was too far away.

I looked over toward Nana's cottage, and that was also too far. Lucky for me, the stream provided enough sound so that most of my movements went unheard by the momma bear. If she spotted me, she would charge me and rip me end from end. I would be shredded girl-burger meat. I wasn't ready to be eaten alive.

Minutes turned into what seemed like hours before the momma and her cubs were out of sight. My stomach was now growling like a grizzly. But the relief that flooded my whole body was a welcome feeling.

When I got to Aunt Esther's I told her all about it.

"Oh my word, Grace! You must be careful! You could have been eaten alive. Now what would your momma do if she had lost you, too? No more taking that tippy toe trail down here, you hear me? You come down the driveway like you're supposed to."

"Yes, ma'am," I said as she was sipping on some hot lemon water. "Where's Alice?"

"She went into town to pick up some groceries and what not." Aunt Esther took another steamy gulp.

"Does Alice know that you have cancer?"

Aunt Esther spit out her hot honey lemon water. "Geez Louise! Why do you always ask me jarring questions when I have a mouth full of hot stuff?" she half smiled as she scolded me.

"I'm sorry." I handed her a napkin and wiped up the droplets that had landed on the coffee table.

"Yes."

At first I didn't know what she was saying "yes" to, but then I understood. Alice knew that Aunt Esther had cancer. Guess that made two, I mean three of us, if you count Aunt Esther. Aunt Esther had gotten much better after the midnight magic did its trick, but she had lost a lot of weight and didn't look as vibrant as she had before she fell ill.

"Is it cancer that is making you sick now?" I asked.

Aunt Esther shrugged. "Alice thinks so."

I wasn't sure what to say next. I tried to think of a way to fix Aunt Esther. I tried to think of something, anything that might work. "What about the midnight magic? That seemed to help, right?"

"Yes, it did."

"What about going to go see a doctor?"

Aunt Esther's face changed from peaceful

to obstinate. "I don't trust doctors. Let's change the subject. Are you excited about school starting on Monday?"

It was only two days away ... *Poop*. I was *not* excited about school starting. "I don't trust school."

Aunt Esther gave me a look like she was shocked but impressed. "Touché," she said. "I guess we are at an impasse. Neither one of us wants any help to get better, sounds kind of stupid when you think about it."

"Aren't doctors there to help you?" I asked.

"They try, but I guess it all depends on whether the patient is open to their treatment."

I started to think about the thought of losing Aunt Esther, and I began to get teary. The thought of Nana being gone *and* Aunt Esther dying was too much to handle. A drop drizzled down my cheek.

"Oh, honey! What's the matter, Grace?" Aunt Esther grabbed my hand.

I flung myself into her embrace and sobbed. "I don't want you to die! Please don't die! I'll miss you too much!" I babbled that and more as I bawled.

Aunt Esther held me, stroking my hair as she consoled me. After the sniffling and hiccupping kicked in, Aunt Esther said, "How about this, if you go to school with an open mind, ready to learn, I'll go to see a doctor."

I pulled back and looked her in the eye. "Kay," I sniffly said. I would do anything, even go to school if that meant Aunt Esther would live longer.

"I've actually been meaning to talk to you and your momma about something."

"What?"

"Remember how I told you that I used to have trouble reading when I was young because of my dyslexia?"

"Yes." I exhaled. "My teachers just think I'm dumb," I said.

"Why do you say that?"

"Because they give me bad grades on things, but to me, I thought I was right, but I wasn't, I guess." That queasy feeling that I got while reading came back to me as I remembered trying to be a good student. I always tried to be good at everything I did but ... "I guess I just don't know how to be a good student and it makes me feel dumb."

"Grace, you are *not* dumb. Remember how you sewed all those incredible outfits for everyone and how you made the RV pillow for me and Alice? And how you threw the best party this town has seen in decades for your nana? And how you made that beautiful sign for Mr. Box? A dumb person couldn't do all that. Heck, an average normal person couldn't do all that." Aunt Esther took a hold of my hands and held them in such a way that made me feel like she was about to tell me something extra important. Her eyes were welling up with emotion as she said, "Grace, *you* are **AMAZING**! And don't you ever forget that."

AMAZING GRACE NEWTON

❧ Twenty-Three ❧

The Russian

Momma woke us up early so that we could drive into town to get some new clothes for the first day of school. Everyone knows that you can't show up on the first day of school in clothes that you had worn before. It was practically a sin. Momma had her coupons ready and her checkbook handy for a shopping spree at the Cmart that was about thirty minutes away from home. This was a big deal, and we kids were extra excited.

We bounced down the driveway and rolled along the country roads until we got to the big town of Asheville. There you could buy all kinds of whatever you wanted, but my Momma knew her way around Cmart green light fashions more than anyone on the planet.

Momma sifted, sorted, and held up clothes in front of us to see if they would fit. Then after a generous pile was formed, we each tried on our various ensembles. I looked great in this super-fun pink romper. I twirled around in front of the mirror for my momma to inspect.

"Oh, yes. That is adorable. Let's definitely get that. Abel how are those pants fitting?"

Abel walked out of the dressing room in a pair of corduroys that hung a few inches too long.

"You know, at the rate that you are growing, I think that we should get those even though they're a tad big," Momma scrutinized while Able shrugged his shoulders then went back to try on more clothes.

Hope walked out wearing a pair of white overalls and a flowery scallop-collared shirt. "What do you think?" she asked Momma.

"Oh! Yes! You look marvelous. Those are on

sale so we should definitely get them," Momma said.

It was fun watching Momma get so excited about our new clothes. I hadn't seen her this happy in months.

"What about you, Momma? Aren't you going to get anything?" I asked. "Don't you want some new clothes?"

"Oh, Grace. That is so sweet of you to ask, but I'm good. I just need y'all to look nice, and that will make me look great.

After we each found a few outfits, we took them to the check out, and Momma presented her coupons. The checkout lady looked at the paper pile then gave my momma a certain look. Momma returned the look with a smile.

In some far away accent, the lady said, "I like your collection of coupons. I am very impressed."

Momma smiled, "Well thank you. I work hard to save money wherever I can."

I looked at the lady's name tag that spelled out M-i-k-a and wondered where her strong accent was from.

After Momma saved tons of money by spending a little on our new clothes, we took our bags from the lady.

"Thank you shopping at Cmart, goodbye, *proshchay*," the lady said in a thick accent.

"Huh?" I asked myself but I guess it was out loud.

The lady smiled and said, "That mean goodbye in Russian."

"Oh!" I had never heard someone speak in another language besides English. "Proshchay," I tried to repeat back.

The lady's eyebrows perked up as she said, "Wow! Very nice. I sink you vill be good Russian speakers one day."

"Thank you," I said.

"Pozhaluysta, that mean you're welcome," she said.

Abel zoomed out of the lane and ran for outside. Momma grabbed my hand and said, "Gotta go!"

• • •

I took my new clothes out of the bag and held them on the way home. I liked the smell of newness in the fabric. I flattened the shirt and stared at the little strawberries that decorated the garment. I looked at the perfect seams— much better than mine. I decided I would work harder on straightening my lines. Hope opened her window letting a blast of warm air brush over my body. My hair floated around my head as if gravity had been suspended when suddenly everything went black.

❧ *Twenty-Four* ❧

Hope's Prayer

"Oh my God! Oh my God! Oh my God!" Hope was crying out as she saw her family unconscious inside her Aunt Esther's flipped over, barely recognizable Jeep. The black twisted metal was being ripped open by emergency responders. The man who was driving the tractor trailer that smashed into them hung his head in shame, but Hope couldn't feel sorry for him right now. All Hope could think about was to ask for God's help. She wasn't a believer until it was her only hope for saving her family. She prayed in a way that she didn't know was possible.

Witnessing the many prayers by her nana as well as other people around her must have punctured her agnostic heart. "Please Lord. Please Lord, save my family. Please help them. Please Lord. They need you to help them. They need you. They need you," she sobbed.

A fireman was performing some tests on Hope to see if she needed care. Hope was too lost in her prayers to notice his attention. He decided, based on the wreckage that she should be taken to the hospital as well as the rest of her family.

"On three!" she heard a man in the distance say. When she opened her eyes, Hope saw four men pull her mother's body from the wreckage.

"Momma!" Hope cried as the men put Ruth Newton's limp body on a gurney and into the ambulance. Blood covered her mother's face. "Momma!"

"We need to get this one to the hospital STAT," the man said. "She's losing a lot of blood, and I can't stabilize her."

They quickly put Ruth Newton inside the ambulance then drove away leaving Hope to watch them remove her younger broken brother and sister. Hope's tears streamed down her face. She had never seen her family so helpless. Awful thoughts ran through Hope's mind. What if they died? She quickly changed her mind-set and refocused on her prayers. She would not allow for that horrible thought to become a reality.

She fell to her knees on the side of the road, looked up into the sky, and clasped her hands together as she cried out. "Please Lord, if I only ever ask one thing of you, please let it be that you would let them live. Please Lord, let them live and heal them. Heal them wholly. Let not a single cell be damaged." Hope visualized the internal organs of her family's bodies, seeing them move in harmony, but then there was a disruption. Hope prayed for an intervention from the maker of all things to come down and lay healing hands upon their wounds. She visualized a complete healing and continued praying for it to be so.

"Hope, would you like to ride with your brother and sister? They could use your prayers along the way," the EMT said.

Hope opened her eyes and saw a man who resembled all the pictures she'd ever seen of

Jesus, all except for the beard. This man had a stubble that made a dark outline around his jaw, but it wasn't filled in. He held his hand out to her and asked, "Would you follow me?" His eyes sparkled like wind on water.

"Yes, Lord." Hope's heavy feeling faded away as she took his hand and followed him.

"Oh, my name is Jason," he blushed.

"I'm Hope," she said to him as she hopped into the ambulance but then remembered that he had just called her by her name. How did he know, she wondered?

"Yes, you are." The man winked before closing the doors.

AND THE MISSING NOODLE

ᔆ *Twenty-Five* ᔆ

The Void

Time went into a warp where nothing existed. I can't describe what I saw because there was nothing. All I know is that I went into some kind of void and didn't leave it for what felt like a million years. Out of the darkness, a tiny sparkle appeared. I heard a soft sound hovering above me. A rusty cardinal flew up and landed in my palm. It began to chirp softly, singing a song. It stood up tall then spread its wings, ready to fly. When it flew up, it became

Pixie Nana flying like she had when she visited me before the boogie barn party.

"Nana!" I said. "Where are we?"

"Oh Grace," she began but looked sad. "You're in between."

"Where's Between?"

"Neither here, nor there," she said and even though it was difficult to understand, I did.

"What should I do?" I asked.

"You need to go there." She pointed behind me.

I looked and saw a tiny speck of light.

"Go, follow that light."

I would do whatever Nana told me to do. So, I did as she said.

❧ *Twenty-Six* ❧

Back From Beyond

A soft light was shining into my lids. It was beginning to get brighter, and I could hear some hushed voices getting louder. "Is she waking up? Grace, can you hear me?" I heard Aunt Esther ask.

I blinked my eyes open but had to close them right away, the light was too bright. I tried to turn my head, but it hurt.

"Don't try to move your head, Grace. It's in a special brace," I heard Alice say.

I lifted my arms up to touch my face but it was blocked by a large metal contraption. What was going on?

I began to panic. What was happening to me?

"Grace, honey, you're okay." Aunt Esther took my hands into hers and softly, yet surely, spoke. "You, Hope, Abel, and your momma were in a car crash. It's a miracle you survived at all! A tractor trailer t-boned my jeep, but you all survived … not without a couple of broken bones and what not, but you're all okay. You just need some time to heal."

I looked at Aunt Esther who almost looked like she did before she became ill. "Are you healed from cancer?" I croaked.

Aunt Esther smiled and laughed, but then tears choked her up. "You're always concerned about other people." She held and petted my hand. "I swear, Grace, you are one of a kind." She sniffed. "Well, I did what I promised you. I went to see a doctor and under her care, I am feeling much better. The treatment she has me on is not as scary as I imagined it would be. Science has come a long way when it comes to cancer treatments."

Papa walked in. "Is she awake?"

"Yes!" Alice proclaimed.

"Oh! Thank you, Jesus!" he said as he grabbed my knee and stood beside me.

"Where's Momma, Hope, and Abel?" I asked with my scratchy voice.

"You must be thirsty," Aunt Esther said as she held up a cup filled with ice-cold water. I sipped from the straw and let the coolness refresh my innards.

"Abel is a floor down from here. Hope is down there with him, and your momma is on the top floor."

"Are they okay?"

Aunt Esther filled me in. "Abel broke a bone in both of his legs and he had something that the doctors were concerned about at first, but he is now more than stable and will make a full recovery."

"What were they concerned about?"

"He lost his loose tooth," Aunt Esther kept a straight face while she joked.

I tried to smile, but it hurt.

"Hope seemed to have floated safely away before the crash because she had absolutely no damage. You and your Momma took the biggest hit. But both of you should also make a full and complete recovery."

Hope walked in. Her eyes bulged in disbelief. "Grace! You're awake!" She ran over and barged between Aunt Esther and Papa saying, "Oh! I'm so happy! You're awake! It's an answered prayer!"

Wait a second. Was I hearing things correctly? "Huh? You prayed?"

Hope looked sheepish, "Yeah, I guess when all else fails, you do what you must in order to save the people you love."

I must have been smiling because everyone reflected my gesture back to me.

"Thank you, Hope," I said.

"You already look so much better, Grace!" Papa said. "I bet you'll be ready to go home in no time."

"We'll see about that," a man wearing a white coat said as he walked in.

"Hello, Grace. I'm Dr. Niles and I've been keeping a close eye on your progress. You were pretty banged up when you came in here but I must say, I have never witnessed anyone heal so quickly. You must have a lot of people caring for you."

"We've been praying a lot," Hope said proudly.

The doctor gave her a superficial smile. I

knew that look. Hope used that one on me plenty of times.

"Can I see Momma and Abel?" I blurted.

The doctor scrunched his face.

"I'm sure we can arrange for something soon, right Doc?" my papa said as he gave the stiff man a pat on the back.

"We'll see what we can do," the doctor said.

AMAZING GRACE NEWTON

⌒ Twenty-Seven ⌒

You're What???

Eventually, I was able to go see Momma. They moved Abel up to her room so they could be together. When they wheeled me in, Abel sat up and said, "Can I have a turn?"

"In what?"

"The wheelchair! That looks fun!"

Obviously Abel was on the fast track to recovery, but Momma didn't look as good. In fact, she looked like she was about to get sick. Actually, she did get sick. She threw up in the trash can that Papa grabbed and held up to her mouth just in time.

"Momma!" I cried out. Even though she was throwing up, I couldn't help but notice the black and blue marks on her face. She looked beaten up. Poor Momma.

Papa cleaned her up as she sat back and tried to look better. He gave her a cup of ice chips to help with her nausea.

"Momma," I softly said wanting to come close to her but not wanting to harm her in the process.

"Come here, honey. I feel better now," Momma said as she gestured with her hands for me to come.

"Momma, why are you sick? Is there something wrong on the inside of you?"

Momma smiled and looked over at Papa who gave her an extra special look of love. "No, Grace. Actually something really right is going on inside of me."

I was confused. What could it be? Because Momma looked kind of terrible but also kind of not terrible. I was confused, to say the least.

"Grace, I'm pregnant!"

"Huh?" What the heck? I was not expecting that! My eyes popped out of my skull as I looked for a baby bump on Momma.

"Yup, just a couple months but yup, I'm pregnant. You're going to be a big sister!"

I looked over at Abel who had one thing on his mind … how to get a ride on this wheelchair. "I think I already am," I said.

Momma and Papa laughed. "Well, you're going to be an even bigger sister!" Papa said.

I wasn't sure how to react, but since they were happy about this news, so was I … I guess.

⊷ *Twenty-Eight* ⊷
The Sibling Slumber Party

After a couple more weeks in the stiff, sterile hospital, we were finally all home. Alice and Aunt Esther made it a point to take on the role of Momma's duties while Hope happily assisted. Abel made the quickest recovery while Momma and I needed a little extra time. But when I got better, it was all the way. We, including me, became super excited about the new baby growing in Momma's belly while Papa was busy building a new room onto our tree house.

"What are we going to name the baby?" I asked.

"We?" Momma asked as if we kids had no say in the matter.

"Yeah! Can we name the baby?" Abel and I looked at each other with excitement brewing in our eyes.

"What did you have in mind?" Momma acted as if she was playing along.

Hmmmm. I thought for a few seconds, "If it's a girl, can we name her Opal?"

Momma's eyebrows rose. She didn't seem to hate the name. "What if it's a boy?"

Papa walked in, grabbed a piece of bacon, and said, "We'll call him Rumin."

Abel and I looked at each other. "Huh?" I asked.

"It's our names put together, Ruth and Lumin." Papa smiled as Momma shook her head. Papa took a couple more pieces of bacon, kissed Momma, then went back to building.

"I think you kids are ready to go to school tomorrow," Momma said as we were eating some breakfast. "I don't want you falling too far behind."

Abel and I had missed the first six weeks of school, and, normally, that should have made me happy but not under such dreadful circumstances.

"But," I began.

"No buts!" Momma resolutely said.

My shoulders dropped. I looked over at Abel who was looking at me like I was a baby. He twisted his fists over his eyes and said, "Wah!"

Hope walked in and said, "I have an idea! How about we have a sibling slumber party tonight?"

"What's that?" I asked.

"It's where we make a big blanket fort in my room, and then we all sleep in there tonight … you know to get you ready for school!"

"Can we Momma?" I asked. "Please?"

"I don't see how that will be getting you ready for school?"

"Please, Momma!" Abel and I begged.

Momma seemed to be going back and forth in her head. "Only if you don't stay up too late! Lights out by 9:00 PM, agreed?"

"Yes ma'am," Abel and I said.

"Hope?" Momma said.

"Yes ma'am."

"Let's go set it up right now!" I began to hobble upstairs.

"Actually," Hope stopped us in our tracks with a thoughtful look wandering over her face. "Let's wait until after supper. I have a few things I need to get finished before we set that up. Besides, you should go outside and play. It's so pretty out!" Hope pointed out the window.

I peeked out of the kitchen window; it did appear to be quite nice. Hope was a new person after the accident. It was as if she liked me or something. She even liked Abel, too. I slowly stepped down the stairs then walked outside. Abel zoomed past me and disappeared to who knows where.

Fall was beginning, filling the slightly smoky air with seasonal scents. It smelled like campfires and storytelling, my favorite fragrance. The breezes lifted my hair, twisting my tendrils into macramé. When I walked over to see Mazie, her hair was messy, too. It must be the autumn wind playing with everybody.

"Hi Mazie!"

"Hi Grace!"

"Are you feeling better?"

"Yes, all except for the fact that I have to go to school tomorrow."

"Didn't we talk about this already?" Mazie asked.

"Yes, but …" I began.

"No, buts, you are going to be just fine!" she said surely.

"You sound like my Momma."

"Your Momma must be very smart," Mazie winked.

"Huh?" I looked up and saw Momma standing beside my purple puddle. "Hi! Momma," I nervously said even though I had no idea why I would be nervous. Maybe having someone witness me talking to Mazie made me feel strange, like I was doing something I shouldn't.

"Mind if I join you?"

I looked back at Mazie who seemed to think it was okay.

"Sure! Want to sit here?" I piled up some fallen leaves to make a comfortable seat for Momma.

With her baby bump growing bigger every day, it was more difficult to do the basic task of sitting but she managed to eventually get herself down to the ground. She looked around at the apple tree canopy above us and the puddle beside us then said, "This is such a nice place to sit. I can see why you're out here so much."

I smiled, feeling complimented at my choice spot to ponder.

"I talked to Aunt Esther, and she thinks that you may have a special need as far as reading is concerned. She thinks you may be dyslexic like she is … or was." Momma shook her head and shrugged. "Anyhow, I called a specialist to have you evaluated, and you are going to meet him tomorrow at school. He runs a program at school to help other kids who have this same problem."

"I have a problem? What's wrong with me?"

Momma must have read the hurt on my face because she grabbed me and gave me a big momma bear hug. "No, not a problem … it's actually a difference. You have a learning difference. And Dr. Conway knows just how to help you learn how to have fun reading as opposed to how you might feel now."

I thought it over. It would be nice to not hate school. It would also be nice to be able to finally make sense of letters and words and such. So I guess it wasn't a bad idea to get some help with learning how to read. Hopefully, Dr. Conway was nice.

"Ruth!" I heard Papa call from the addition that he had been busy hammering. "Can you come here a minute?"

Momma struggled to stand then looked back at me. "Want to come or stay?"

"I'll stay here."

"Okiedokie," Momma said as she walked away.

After a couple quiet minutes, I walked over to the chicken coop to check on Noodle, who was missing, as usual. All the other nameless chickens were happily pecking away at various bugs or seeds. Just as I was wondering, Smith and Wesson rode up on their bikes with Noodle riding in the front basket—a plastic milk crate.

"Noodle! What are you doing in there?" I saw Noodle comfy as can be, all gussied up in one of Miss Josie's dresses, sitting in the crate lined in a fluffy ragged blanket.

"She goes everywhere with us!" Wesson bragged.

I kind of felt envious of the bond Noodle had adopted with the twins. Maybe I didn't pay enough attention to her? Maybe she just liked the boys better?

"We just wanted to make sure she was okay since you was in that accident, and all," Smith said sensing my dismay.

I couldn't rightfully be mad at them for taking care of my chicken when I had been gone so much. "No, actually, thank you for looking after her, I guess." I petted the top of Noodle's head as she quietly clucked. She stood up as if she was going to jump out but then sat back down letting out an egg.

"You wanna ride bikes with us?" Wesson asked.

At first I wasn't sure if I could remember how. But then I decided today was a good day to relearn, if need be. I hurried over to the barn and wheeled out Princess Leia.

"Tires need some air," Smith said. "You got a pump?"

I set down the kickstand then went back in for the tire pump.

Wesson got right to work making sure both of my tires had plenty of air. I twisted the valve covers, threw my leg over the seat, then followed Smith, Wesson, and Noodle around the green hills for the afternoon.

The fireflies began to blink, indicating our time to go home. When they brought me home safely, Smith asked, "You wanna take Noodle for the night?"

I looked at Noodle proudly sitting in the crate and couldn't take her from them. They were like the three musketeers. "No, I think she's your Noodle now." I leaned over and gave her a peck.

"Well, we'll come see you tomorrow after school, kay?" Wesson said as they pedaled away.

"Kay," I said as I waved goodnight.

AMAZING GRACE NEWTON

❦ *Twenty-Nine* ❦
The Hurry and The Worry

I rushed inside because I wanted to make sure that we had time to set up for the sibling slumber party.

Aunt Esther, Alice, and everybody were all busy getting dinner ready when I walked in.

"Grace! Where have you been? I was worried sick!" Momma asked as she was taking some things out of the refrigerator. Momma still walked and worked much slower since the accident but probably more so because she was pregnant. Momma never seemed to care before when I stayed out till almost dark so I wasn't sure what was different now.

"I was just riding bikes with Smith and Wesson."

"Told you," Hope said.

"Well, still, next time come tell me when you decide to take off."

"Yes, ma'am," I said.

"Now, can you help Hope set the table?"

I really wanted to get ready for the sibling slumber party, but I knew that when Momma asked us to do these kinds of things¾chores, there was no going around it.

After everyone gathered around the table for supper. Hope asked, "May I say grace?"

Everyone looked a little shocked, especially me as Hope asked for a blessing on our food as well as for all of us.

"Thank you, Hope," Momma said as she picked up her napkin and set it on her lap.

Besides Hope finding God, Abel now ate real food like pot roast, maple brussels sprouts, corn casserole, and cinnamon applesauce, voluntarily—which, by the way, might be my new favorite meal. Momma seemed to be back to her old self before Nana had died …

but possibly somewhat even better because of Papa's excitement over the new baby. He tenderly placed his hand on her belly and gave her a kiss which caused her to blush. Aunt Esther had a healthy glow about her, and Alice was strong as always.

I got lost in the fullness of family dinnertime … not just the warm feeling of togetherness but the delightful tastes that were put together with love. Each bite was rich with taste. I was enjoying my food so much that I almost stopped obsessing over our slumber party. But then my mind returned to its one track. "Can we go get ready for the sibling slumber party right after supper? I want to have enough time to build the blanket fort." I smiled, hoping to encourage a positive response from Momma and Papa.

"Sure, right after you finish with the dishes," Momma said.

"Oh, man!" I said disappointed.

"We'll have plenty of time," Hope said. "Don't worry."

I took a deep breath and finished my dinner. Everyone else was taking much too long to finish eating. I was tapping my fork on my plate hoping that would hurry everyone along, but no, all it resulted in was Momma glaring at me, telling me to ***Stop that Incessant Tapping!***

"Don't worry," Aunt Esther said. "Alice and I will help you get those dishes done in a flash."

I gave Aunt Esther a smile and said to her and Alice, "Thank you."

AND THE MISSING NOODLE

✿ Thirty ✿

Papa's Horse "Tale"

The grandfather clock chimed seven times. Finally, we were finished cleaning the kitchen, and it was already much too late, if you asked me. We would never be able to build the kind of magical blanket fort that I had in mind *and* have enough time to enjoy it before we had to go to sleep. I kind of gave up on the whole idea so that I wouldn't be too disappointed. I guess Hope picked up on my despair as I slumped onto the couch.

"Hey, Grace and Abel, come follow me. I have something to show you," she said. I didn't care to see anything other than what we now could not do, but I didn't want to sound like a brat so I followed Hope and Abel up to her room.

When she opened the door, I almost fell to the floor. Hope had already constructed the most magical, glowing, awe-inspiring, enchanted blanket fort ever. Twinkly lights, purposefully spaced, illuminated the darkened room making it appear like we were in outer space. From inside the fort, strings of lights made the blankets appear aglow. I couldn't wait to go inside.

"Can we go in?" I asked.

"Yes!" Hope said. "Go!"

Abel and I scrambled inside the blanket fort and found three puffy beds in a shape that resembled flower petals waiting for us. The beds were made out of piles of pillows, sleeping bags, and sheets. Abel jumped onto what would be his bed as I flopped back onto one of the beds and asked, "How did you do all of this?"

"I learned a thing or two from my little sister and brother," she said.

"From us?" Abel looked shocked that Hope could learn anything from us.

I thought back to the time Abel and I had made the pretend space shuttle for Hope. We did a pretty good job, if I do say so myself, but this blanket fort was beyond fantastic. Everything was precise in its place. I could see Hope's perfectionism in every detail like the bunches of flowers wrapped in ribbon in each corner, the lights so carefully strung, and the perfect pleats of the blankets. After closing her bedroom door, she pulled the grandly tethered opening to the blanket fort shut.

"I forgot Milkshake," Abel said as he sat up. "I'll be right back." Abel ducked under the blankets then went out of the room.

I forgot Lumps, too. I also forgot to brush my teeth and get in my pajamas. "I'll be right back, too," I said as I followed Abel. I quickly did my nighttime routine then reminded Abel to do so as well when I saw him walking back with Milkshake.

"We're back!" I announced as we walked back into our sibling slumber party.

"It's about time," Hope yawned. "I was beginning to get sleepy."

""Who wants to tell the first story?" Hope asked.

"I do!" said Papa from outside the blanket

fort. He peeked in and saw us all snuggled up in our beds. "Permission to come in?" he asked.

"Okay, but only for one story," Abel said.

"Well, okay, but the story I have to tell is about Milkshake, okay?"

"Okay," Abel giggled.

Papa made the blanket fort a lot cozier when he got in. By cozy, I mean smaller. After he settled in next to Abel and me, he began to tell the story of how Milkshake got shook.

"Long, long time ago, see, there once was a baby horse who was born to a fine young filly named Shakira. But we'll talk more about that baby in a bit. Shakira shook like no other horse in the world, but all her talent was going to waste. She wanted to be in the rodeo bucking those cowboys off her back like the best of the rodeo horses do, but since rodeo horses are male, it wasn't allowed. The star horse of the rodeo was named The Milky Way because his coat looked like a star-speckled galaxy."

"Shakira spent days and nights watching the rodeo, wishing that she could get in the ring but nope, she was never allowed. She watched The Milky Way thrill the crowds with his impressive bucking skills. The Milky Way could sense Shakira watching him and thought it was because he was so handsome. He was indeed handsome, but that's not why Shakira was watching him. She watched how he used his strength and agility to throw the men off of his back."

"One day as The Milky Way was in the middle of an impressive routine, he fell back wrong and broke his leg. This was a career ending injury for The Milky Way but more importantly, it was a life-ending injury. When horses break their legs, it's very common for the owner to shoot the horse due to the potential risks of infection that the leg could get resulting in a natural, much more painful death, anyway."

"But back at the stable, as the man raised a gun to shoot The Milky Way, Shakira shook her way out of her pen and got between the gun and The Milky Way. Baffled, the man put down the gun and left the two horses alone. After that day, no one could get near The Milky Way to shoot him without Shakira threatening to kick them. Shakira's and The Milky Way's owner persuaded the men to leave them be. But to also do everything they could to mend The Milky Way's leg. Eventually, with the constant guard and care of Shakira, The Milky Way made a complete recovery. But what was even better, they also fell in love. When Shakira became pregnant with their foal, they decided on the perfect name, Milkshake. And that's where Milkshake came from, Shakira and The Milky Way," Papa said in a summed up manner.

"Did you just make that up?" Hope asked.

Papa laughed and said, "Maybe."

"That's pretty unbelievable," Hope said.

"I believe you, Papa," Abel said as he turned to him while brushing Milkshake's brown fur.

"No, I'm saying it's pretty unbelievable how you just made that all up. You're a great story-teller."

"How do you know it's a story?" I asked, being a little stinker.

"Because we're talking about a stuffed horse, for crying out loud!"

"But this horse is based on a real one!" Papa joked.

"Oh, okay," Hope shook her head.

"Who's turn is it next?" Abel asked.

"To do what?" Hope wondered.

"Tell a story," he answered.

"I think you should each take a turn then time for lights out," Papa said.

"Can you go again, Papa?" I asked. "I don't have a good story like yours."

"Nope. You just have to use your imagination and then fill in the spaces with your words." Papa stood to go. "In my absence, I nominate Hope to go next." He turned to leave then looked back and said, "Goodnight!"

"Goodnight, Papa!" we all said.

None of our stories were nearly as creative as Papa's, but we still had fun giggling the night away at stupid things like Abel's squeaky armpit farts, and my freaky gurgly belly, and Hope's flaring nostrils.

AMAZING GRACE NEWTON

ᦕ *Thirty-One* ᦖ

School's For . . .

We were snug as bugs all night long, curled up against one another. It was a shame that rooster had to crow so early. Morning comes way too soon when you don't want to wake up. But at least I didn't spend the entire previous evening fretting over having to go to school.

The best thing about our car accident was that our new clothes were virtually undamaged and we were all able to wear them for our first day of school. Actually, Hope had been able to go to school soon after the accident, but Abel and I would be starting about six weeks late. I was afraid that I would have no friends and that I would have missed so much that I would be lost.

Before we left, I ran over to see Mazie.

"Wish me luck," I said.

"Have a great day!" she said. "And good luck," she added for good measure.

Papa drove us in the old red pickup truck. As we bumbled down the quiet country roads, I stuck my head out of the window drying my wet showered hair. It felt good to be clean and in my nice new clothes. I looked down at my romper and decided that we would have a good day just like Mazie had said.

When we got to Apple Valley Elementary, Abel jumped over me then took off running into school like a rocket. He was obviously all healed from his broken bones. I, on the other hand, wasn't as eager.

Papa reached over and patted my hand. "Hey there, you okay?" he asked.

"Yeah," I said as I reached for the handle.

"Did I ever tell you that you are cute as a bunny?"

"Yes," I said knowing where this was headed.

"Did I ever tell you that you are sweeter than a sugar cube?"

"Yes, Papa."

"Did I ever tell you that I love you more than all the stars in the sky?" he reached and pulled me over giving me a loud wet raspberry on my cheek and neck. I giggled and giggled so hard that I forgot that other kids could probably hear the suspect noises leaking out from the truck.

"All right, now you get up in that there school and learn you some cool stuff, you hear me?"

"Yes, Papa," I said as lingering laughter echoed throughout my whole body.

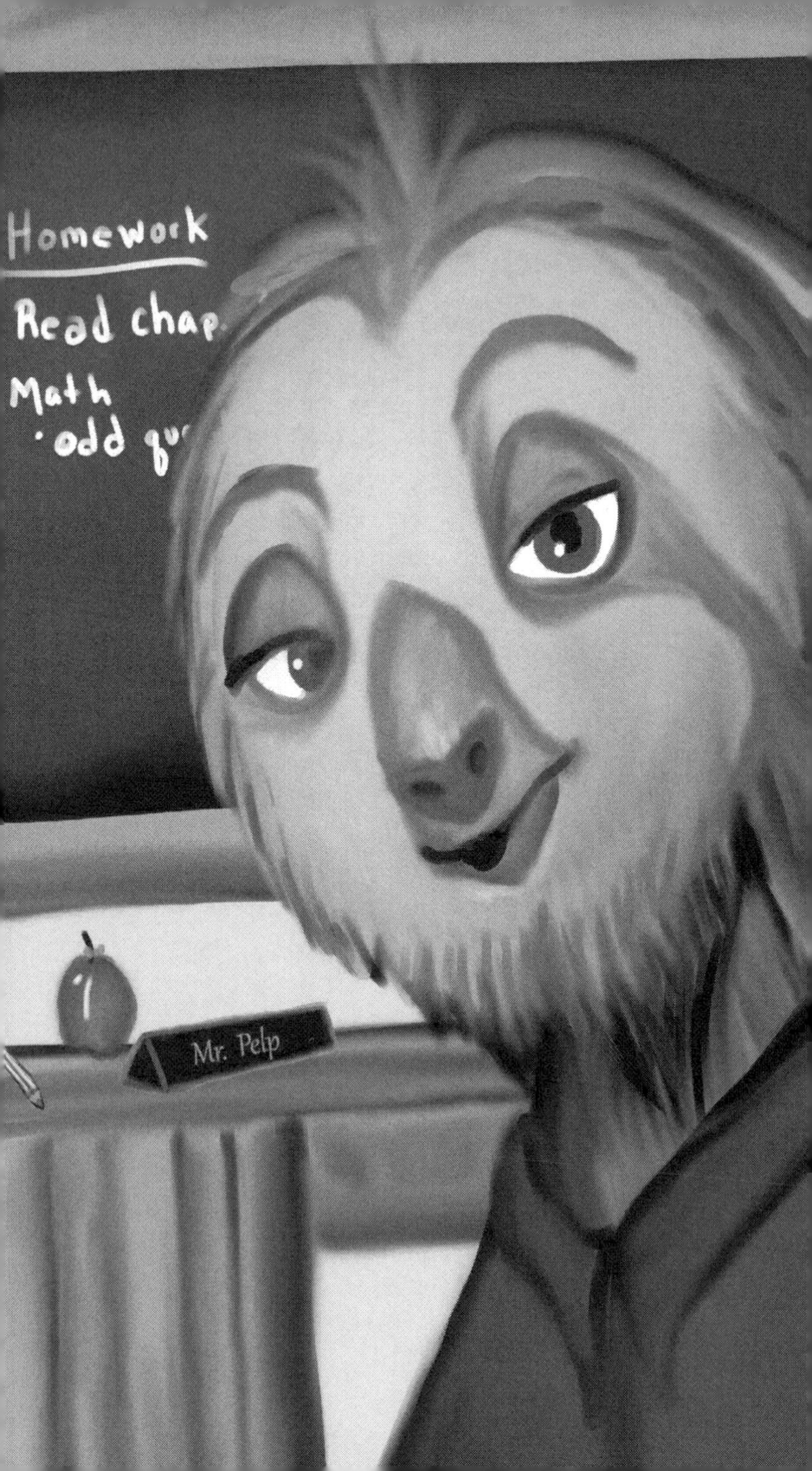
Homework
Read chap.
Math
·odd qu
Mr. Pelp

‹⁀ *Thirty-Two* ⁀›

The Sloth

I could barely walk straight, but I managed to find my new class with the help of the assistant principal, Mrs. Jacobi.

"Mr. Pelp?" Mrs. Jacobi said to the teacher in my new classroom. "I'd like to introduce you to Grace Newton. She was in a terrible car accident and is just now able to return to school. Please help her feel at home as she still might need some time to recover. Students, I would like for you all to make sure that you welcome Grace back. She was in the hospital for a long time."

I had not told Mrs. Jacobi a thing about our accident. I guess she must have heard about it from someone else. Word travels fast in small towns.

"Welcome, Grace. I'm Mr. Pelp and I have a nice seat for you over here." He gestured to a chair in the second row for me to sit. Mr. Pelp was one of the tallest men I had ever seen. I pictured him in the circus walking around on stilts in red and white striped pants. But Mr. Pelp didn't need stilts or the red and white striped pants to appear so tall. He was super tall, but he looked and moved and talked slowly like a sloth—one of my favorite creatures. Mr. Pelp slowly smiled at me before he gradually turned to the blackboard.

"I love your romper," I heard a girl say from behind me. I turned around and found a happy face smiling at me. "Hi!"

"Hi," I quietly whispered.

"I'm Veronique."

"Hi," I said again.

"You're Grace Newton, right?"

"Yeah," I looked around at all the other kids watching us talk. I looked back at the teacher who was still slowly turning to the blackboard.

"I heard all about your terrible accident. I'm glad you're okay," the girl next to me said.

"Thank you," I whispered.

"Yeah, we all heard about it. You must have been pretty banged up," the boy sitting diagonal from me said.

I smiled at him silently acknowledging his guess.

"Did you get any super powers?" another boy who was sitting behind him asked.

"No," I smiled as I shook my head.

"Grace was already amazing," I heard a familiar country accent say. I turned the other way and found Smith Springfield snickering in my direction.

"Smith!" I exclaimed in a louder whisper than I had planned. He grinned from ear to ear.

"Let's keep it down now," Mr. Pelp said as he deliberately wrote something on the blackboard.

I turned my eyes back to the teacher, but my thoughts were happily swimming in my new school life.

AMAZING GRACE NEWTON

✍ Thirty-Three ✍

Genius Alert

Because of my learning difference, when all the other kids went to music class, I went to see Dr. Conway. Today, Mrs. Jacobi took me to his classroom to introduce me.

He was a friendly looking man who reminded me of what I imagined a favorite uncle would be like, if I had one—warm, friendly, and humble.

"Well, hello, Grace! I've heard so much about you. It is a pleasure to finally meet you,"

Dr. Conway said in a formal matter but with such familiarity, it put me at ease. "Please, sit where you'd like."

There were no other kids in the class so I could choose from any number of seats. I picked the closest one then sat. He and Mrs. Jacobi exchanged some words before she went to leave. As she closed the door, she waved her fingers at me. I smiled and waved back.

Dr. Conway gave me a few tests to evaluate my skills. After he was finished tallying up my scores, he clasped his hands together and said, "I have some great news for you."

"What is it?"

"You are incredibly brilliant; I'd say genius level."

"Huh?" He must be mistaken. I knew myself pretty well, and I was certainly no genius. Hope, on the other hand, might be.

"According to these IQ tests, you are at the top tier. You know," he paused, "that means, you have some kind of superpower!"

I gasped. I had no idea that learning about my reading issues would be so much fun.

"But as with all superheroes and geniuses like yourself, it comes at a cost."

"What?" I asked.

"Well, as you probably already know, superheroes have one thing that makes them weak. Achilles had his heal, Superman's was Kryptonite, yours happens to be reading in the form of dyslexia."

"Oh."

"Don't fret. That's just a simple reading insufficiency, but because you are so brilliant *and* I'm such a super duper doctor," he paused and smiled in a prideful manner for dramatic effect. "You will be able to overcome this and not only read well, you'll also do great in all of your classes." Dr. Conway smiled, assuring me of my prognosis. "Are you ready to get your superpower?"

"Yes!"

๑ *Thirty-Four* ๑

Fooper!

Last year, as well as the one before it, I was a submarine student, meaning my grades were below C level. So, to have Dr. Conway say that I was a genius was pretty unbelievable. Was I smarter now? Maybe the doctor tightened some of my loose screws when I was in that accident?

At lunch it seemed as if everyone was trying to sit next to me. Maybe it was because of Smith and Wesson being so popular and them being my best friends. But either way, I finally understood how Hope and Abel seemed to feel about school. It wasn't so bad. In fact, it was fun, but don't tell anyone I said that!

Abel found me waiting in the parent pick-up line.

"Hi Grace! When's Papa gonna get here?"

I shrugged because his guess was as good as mine.

Smith and Wesson pedaled over and said, "Why didn't you ride Princess?"

"You mean Leia?"

"Yeah, you should ride with us," they suggested.

"Isn't it a long ride?"

"Not how the crow flies."

"Huh?" I crinkled my face not understanding their terminology.

"We gotta secret short cut," Smith said.

"Oh! I'll ask my parents if I can."

"Can I, too?" Abel asked.

"Not sure if you can keep up," Wesson said as if Abel couldn't outrun us on our bikes.

Abel and I laughed. "He might be small, but he is mighty fast," I assured them.

"There's Papa!" Abel said as he took off.

The twins tried hard to not look impressed with Abel's speed.

"See y'all later? You going to bring Noodle over for a visit, right?" I asked.

"Sounds like a plan," Smith said.

"10-4," Wesson said trying to sound grown up.

"Toot-a-loo!" I said before walking away.

On the way home, as Papa, Abel, and I traveled along the dusty roads, I thought about my day and was actually excited about returning tomorrow. I couldn't wait to get home to tell everyone what I was currently telling Papa.

As soon as Papa parked the pickup, Momma opened the door for me and asked me how my day was. I told her how I had a superpower but how I also had a Kryptonite and that my real teacher was a sloth and how everyone was so nice and that I couldn't wait to go back. I think I may have said all that in one breath.

Momma looked so happy. Then Aunt Esther came in and asked me to repeat everything I had just told Momma. Then Alice asked me to do the same ... and then at dinner Hope needed to hear the story as well. At first I enjoyed having everyone's attention as they listened to my recounting of the day, but after repeating it over and over, I was tired of hearing it myself.

"Hope, how was your day?" I asked, ready to hear someone else's voice for a change.

"Exactly as I had wished—normal. Sometimes having everything normal is nice. I never appreciated normal until recently."

"Amen to that," Alice said while giving Hope a wink.

"Abel, how about you? How was your day?" Momma asked.

"Fooper!" he said with his mouth full of food.

"Super?" Momma asked.

He nodded as we all laughed.

Papa said in his deep deliberate voice, "What a blessing today has been. I am over-abundantly grateful for my *Fooper* family." He smiled and gave Abel's hair a good ruffling.

After dinner and dishes, I remembered that Smith and Wesson forgot to come by with Noodle. They must have had something else to do. Yawning, I peeked outside to see if maybe I had missed them. I saw a little sparkle reflect from the moonlight over my purple puddle.

I stepped off the porch and followed the moon's shine over to the puddle. There was a familiar sensation buzzing around me, but I knew it wasn't an insect. It felt like a spirit visiting.

"Nana?" I looked up but didn't see her flying around. The sky was a deep dark purple with light puffy violet clouds hanging around the moon. I wondered why they weren't moving. Maybe they had nowhere else to be? I looked back down and over the edge of the puddle. Just like the first time I had found this magical bog, it reflected the purple sky and clouds above me. Right in front of my freckled face, I found Mazie looking back with a smile bigger than mine.

"Well," she asked. "How was it?"

I thought about the millions of times I had told the whole story of my day then decided to go with the better, more fitting version and said, "It was amazing."

Nana's Chocolate Chip Cookie Recipe

INGREDIENTS

- 2 ¼ cups all-purpose flour
- 1 teaspoon baking soda
- 1 teaspoon salt
- 1 cup (2 sticks) butter, softened
- ¾ cup granulated sugar
- ¾ cup packed brown sugar
- 1 teaspoon vanilla extract
- 2 large eggs
- 2 cups Nestlé Toll House Semi-Sweet Chocolate Morsels
- 1 cup chopped nuts
- 1 cup toffee bits

DIRECTIONS

- Preheat oven to 375°F.
- Combine flour, baking soda, and salt in small bowl. Beat butter, granulated sugar, brown sugar, and vanilla extract in large mixer bowl until creamy. Add eggs, one at a time, beating well after each addition. Gradually beat in flour mixture. Stir in morsels, toffee, and nuts. Drop by rounded tablespoon onto ungreased baking sheets.
- Bake for 9 to 11 minutes or until golden brown. Cool on baking sheets for 2 minutes. Eat while warm, dunk into fresh milk and taste the yum.

About the Author

N. Jane Quackenbush is a graduate of Palm Beach Atlantic University. She lives in an *Amazing* house filled with kitties and strange art in St. Augustine, FL. After a family trip to North Carolina, Ms. Quackenbush was inspired by the peaceful landscape and the wholesome nature of the area. Amazing Grace Newton personifies the overwhelming emotions such inspirational settings produce.

You can also stay in touch with N. Jane Quackenbush on Facebook.

N. Jane Quackenbush has also written the following Children's Picture Books:
The Rocket Ship Bed Trip
The Pirate Ship Bed Trip
The Afternoon Moon

Middle Grade Books:
The Children's Horrible House
Return to The Children's Horrible House
Escape from The Children's Horrible House

Amazing Grace Newton and The Purple Puddle
Amazing Grace Newton and The RV Trip

If you enjoyed reading *Amazing Grace Newton and The Missing Noodle*, please leave a review.

Made in the USA
Columbia, SC
01 October 2021